MW01656818

DEON

I've been driving for two hours, and I have another forty minutes before I get to our final destination. I'm not sure if Solanie is awake or not. I have her hog tied in the trunk of my car. She's also gagged because I don't know if she's a screamer or not. Anticipation has my hands slick with sweat. It's hard to believe that this is really happening. I've waited so long that it almost feels unreal. Knight King was so close to ruining everything, but I one upped his ass. I wish I could see his face the moment he realizes Solanie is long gone. I laugh so hard that my chest starts hurting.

I send Nate a one-worded text, letting him know what I've finally done, and toss my phone into my empty cup holder. I ease my foot off the gas pedal once I realize I'm almost going forty miles over the speed limit. The last thing I need is for some punk ass cop to pull me over right now. My excitement to get Solanie to our new home has overpowered my common sense. I glance out of my rearview mirror to make sure nobody is behind me.

It was incredibly risky to take Solanie outside of Knight's home. The risk scared me but at the same time turned me the fuck on. I hadn't planned on taking Solanie tonight, but when the opportunity presented itself, I pounced on it.

My mind celebrates my achievement the entire drive. The tension in my shoulders doesn't relax until I pull in front of my new home. I get out of the car and finally exhale.

Home sweet home.

I've been working on this place for an entire year. A secluded cabin looking house beyond the city limits in a wooded area. The streets aren't even paved out here, and the nearest neighbor is over thirty miles away.

It's perfect.

I pop the trunk, and just as I expected, Solanie is awake. Her eyes are wide with terror, and her face is stained with tears that have gone dry.

"Hello, Solanie."

With our eyes locked like this, it's hard to break the moment. Here she is, up close and personal, and all mine.

She narrows her eyes to slits and glares at me in a way that I do *not* like. She shouldn't be looking at me like this. I haven't hurt her *yet*, so the look on her face right now is unwarranted.

I pull her out of the trunk. It's harder than I thought carrying her into the house because she keeps fighting against me. Her fighting is useless because I'm so much stronger than her. All the kicking and writhing she's doing only tires her out. She might as well get used to being here because once I get her inside of our new home, she'll never be able to leave. The house has been perfectly set up to eliminate any attempt at escape. I toss her to the floor and pull a gun from my waistband. I don't point it at her. I just let it rest against my leg. When she sees it, she quickly settles down.

"I'm gonna take the gag out of ya mouth but you bet' not scream. If you do, no one will hear you, but you will suffer the consequences of disobeying me."

I slowly take the gag out of her mouth, and I'm pleased that she doesn't try to scream. Her eyes are on the gun in my hand. I then pull the box cutter from my back pocket and cut the ropes that bind her. As soon as she's freed, she tries to jump on me!

With one sharp blow to the side of her head with the butt of my gun, she lands flat on her back. She yelps out in what sounds like a mixture of pain and terror. I can't remember the last time I heard a more beautiful sound.

"That's the last time you gonna do some shit like that," I warn her.

She starts crying and holding the side of her head. Her lip has split, and blood seeps from the small cut. I didn't mean to do that, but she forced my hand. Even so, I must admit there is nothing more beautiful than the sight of Solanie's blood. The monster inside of me roars to be unleashed on her.

"You're mine now, Solanie." I figure I might as well break it to her now. "You will never leave this house again. Your old life was just that, your old life. This is your new reality. For every action there is a consequence. Obedience is rewarded. Disobedience will be punished. From this moment forward, I own everything about your existence, including whether you live or die."

Her silent tears turn into loud sobs that shake her body. I bite my lip to keep from lashing out at her. Instead of crying, she should be celebrating. Since she's here, The Beauty Butcher will never hunt again.

First thing's first, Solanie needs a bath. I need to scrub every trace of Knight King off her body. She reeks of that nigga, and the thought of him touching her triggers my rage and gives me the urge to do something violent.

I have Solanie now, so I'll deal with Knight at a later time. I can tell the shirt that she's wearing belongs to that nigga, so I rip it from her body. She's completely naked underneath it. My mouth waters at her hardened nipples. I'm captivated by the sight of her, crying and wailing out for God to help her. But I'm also disgusted by the sight of her wrapped in another man's scent. As for now, she needs to be cleansed. Her body, mind, and heart need to be wiped clean of every trace of Knight King because finally Solanie belongs completely to me.

She.

Is.

Mine.

KNIGHT

My knuckles are white from rubbing them so hard. Fire hot rage consumes me to the point I cannot think straight. The only thing on my mind is murder. Bloody, torturous murder. I will paint the city of Houston red if need be until I find who had the unmitigated gall to try *me*.

"Knight, baby, please sit down," my mother says. Her eyes are worried, and her voice is troubled. She knows the thoughts that are running through my head. I stop pacing and sit down, but sitting feels like wasting time, so I'm back on my feet just as fast.

Solanie was only supposed to be running out to the car to get her cell phone, but when two minutes turned into five, I hopped out of bed and came outside to find my car door opened wide, her cell phone on the ground, but no sight of her.

It took a minute for me to process the scene because surely nothing had happened to Solanie. Surely, no one was that out of their mind to come onto my property and take something that belonged to me! Immediately, I called my father while I frantically checked my surveillance cameras. Every inch of my property is under twenty-four monitoring. So imagine my surprise when I rolled back the footage to see things from two months ago being played for me.

It only took fifteen minutes for my parents to show up. Just as I'm about to ask where the fuck are they, Kian and Kaleb come barreling into my house.

"Where have y'all been?" Momma stands up as soon as

they enter my living room.

"Uh, sorry, Ma. We got caught up in some," Kaleb says.

"Something like what?" she wants to know. "What could possibly be more important than this!"

"It doesn't matter, Ma," I say. "They're here now." I don't have time to listen to her go back and forth with my brothers. Not when Solanie is out there... somewhere.

"Who would want to commit suicide this bad?" Kian says. His forehead is creased, and his voice sounds just as confused.

My father hasn't said more than two words since he and Moms arrived. It's always a bad thing when Kurtis King goes silent. Under any other circumstance, this would unease me. But right now, I *need* that side of my father.

Please forgive me. I may have been a bit misleading in my earlier depiction of my family. I know I claimed that after a run in with the law, Kurtis King went all the way straight. That was a lie. He only got smarter, neater, and imperceptible about his shit. My father built a reputation in the streets for his merciless, ruthless, murderous ways. He had a team of niggas that were devoutly loyal to him, niggas that would take a bullet straight in the heart for him. But he always said his most valuable solider was my mother. She was smarter than your average and just as gangsta. There were plenty of nights my father came home knee deep in some street shit and without having to ask, Momma got rid of all the evidence. I was born into this crazy lifestyle, and at an early age, my father groomed me to take over his empire. Growing up with parents like mine was crazy! I caught my first body before I lost my virginity. In elementary school, I knew more about cocaine than I did Shakespeare, Albert Einstein, or Christopher Columbus. Shit was crazy!

My father was an innovator. He went and found men from the poorest of poor towns in countries like Haiti, Cuba, Venezuela, and Honduras and illegally brought them back to the

U.S. He treated them well and paid them even better, thus creating the kind of loyalty the average d-boy would never possess. These men were able to support their families back home in a way they never would have had my father not put them on. They respected my father and loved him for changing every part of their lives.

What I said about the pill clinic was true though. The money we made there was so lucrative, my father was able to leave the game for good. He'd always wanted to get out before death or prison came for him, and he succeeded in that. My father didn't want my younger brothers, Kian and Kaleb, to grow up in the same way I did, so he shielded them from the things I'd witnessed. He'd given them a choice at which route they wanted to take. Kaleb took the straight and narrow, but Kian was more like my father than he wanted to see. Kian is bullheaded with a bloodthirst for murder and power.

I hope you can forgive me for being misleading earlier, but as you may know by now, the feds are watching and sometimes you can't be too careful.

Given my family history, it perplexes me that someone would bring their asses onto my property and fuck with what's mine! My whole family is seated in my living room, and not one of us can think of one person who'd have such a death wish on their lives.

"Whoever did this is smart," Kurtis finally speaks up. He's seated with his chin in his hand and his face solemn. "They've been inside your home, fucked up your surveillance system, all without you even noticing a thing."

I know my father hasn't flat out called me stupid, but his tone says more than what his words just have. I take the silent assault in stride, because he's right. Someone *had* been inside my house and touched my shit without me noticing.

"Maybe we're looking at this all wrong. Perhaps it's not someone who has a vendetta against *us*," Kaleb says. "Maybe it's someone from Solanie's life."

I look at my youngest brother. He's tall and slim, his hair is cut low, he's always clean shaven, and he's wearing the stereotypical glasses that all nerds wear. He's never had to get his hands dirty being a King. He's never even seen an ounce of blow before. He has zero street sense, but nevertheless, he's an asset and what he's just said sounds more realistic than anyone wanting to fuck with a King.

"I thought you had this woman checked out," Momma says. Her eyes are on Kian and me.

"I did," I say. "She's straight laced. She isn't involved with anyone or anything shady."

Kian clears his throat. "Yeah, Knight's right. I did the background myself. The girl is legit."

"You must have missed something then," Kurtis says. "Somewhere in her life is someone who has no idea who he's fucking with or the immensity of what he's just done. She's connected in some kinda way to someone who doesn't know shit about the Kings."

"That ain't possible," Kian argues. "Every fuckin' body either knows the Kings or knows someone who knows what the fuck we're capable of."

"See, that's your fucking problem." Kurtis glowers at Kian. "You think you know every damn thing. You missed something in the background check, and now we're mixed up in some shit that shouldn't even involve us!"

Kian knows better than to say anything more. Our father hardly ever raises his voice, so when he does, we know he's seconds away from spazzing.

Momma begins massaging his shoulders to calm him down. She locks eyes with me and says, "This girl… is she worth going to war over, Knight?"

I don't have to even think about it. "Yeah, Ma."

Momma smiles, and dangerous excitement twinkles in her eyes. She looks at my father, and he smiles back at her. "Well, let's get ready for war, baby!"

Flashes of Solanie's smile pop into my mind. The feel of her body underneath me, the smell of her skin, the way she looks at me as if she can read the secrets of my soul. If I hadn't known before, I know it now. Solanie belongs to me.

I will get her back, and she will be my wife. Whoever stole her out of my driveway will die a long, agonizing death, and she will be right by my side watching the motherfucka bleed out. We will grow old together and build our own empire of little Kings. If I hadn't known before, I know it now. I love that girl.

She.

Is.

Mine.

SOLANIE

There is not an adjective in the English dictionary that can describe the fear that I feel. Never in a million nightmares did I expect something like this would ever happen to me. The man before me is completely out of his mind. I don't know if he's going to kill me, but I can tell by the glassy look in his eyes that he's bat-shit crazy.

The side of my head throbs, but I can't concentrate on the pain. I have to think of a way out of here. I look around the small room for anything I can use as a weapon against this guy. The room looks like any ordinary living room with a tan couch in the center and a wooden worn-out coffee table in front of it. An old school TV with an antenna sitting on top sits on top of a wooden TV stand in the corner. There are no pictures on the walls. A weird looking, thick, black box is on the front door that leads outside of the house.

Oh my God, there are no windows in this place! Not even one. My throat feels as if it's about to close up.

How could this be happening to me? These types of things don't happen to people like me. This is the type of thing that happens in horror movies. My mind goes to all those women that have been recently killed at the hands of the Beauty Butcher. Horror wraps itself around my body until I can barely breathe. My eyes shoot up to the maniac that's staring back at me. Could he be the same evasive killer that the entire police department is looking for? Other than the starry-eyed look he has, nothing about him screams serial killer. He's an average looking dude, probably about five feet eleven, brown skinned, in desperate need of a haircut. Medium build, no distinguishing features. Everything about him is completely average looking. He's the kind of guy you could walk past in the grocery store and five minutes later not be able to describe a thing about him. That's just how average he looks.

"Move your hands," he commands. Greed blazes in the eyes that he hasn't taken off me since we entered this house.

I blink repeatedly. Terror burns through every vein in my body. I feel like I'm going to pass out from the choke hold that fear has on my throat.

"I said move your hands. Don't make me have to tell you a third time. I promise you won't like the consequences, Solanie."

Both of my hands are doing a terrible job at hiding the parts of my body that I don't want him to see. I won't just lay back and let him rape me, so I stare defiantly back at him, welcoming whatever consequences that he's threatening me with. I'm not sure where I find the inner strength to do this, because all of my instincts are yelling for me to do everything he tells me to do.

Yet there's something in my gut telling me to be strong. Maybe it's the shimmer of hope that I've been holding on to since this nightmare began. A small piece of hope keeps telling me that Knight is out there looking for me right now. I was supposed to be back inside his house within two minutes. If Knight is the man that I think he is, he's out there right now searching high and low for me. I pray to God that the police are already on this maniac's trail. I've convinced my mind that rescue is on the way because that's the only way I can cope with what's happening to me right now.

Before I can react, this crazy ass dude has leapt to his feet and is across the room at the speed of light. Both of his hands are around my throat, lifting me to my feet. I struggle to pry his hands away because it feels like he's seconds away from crushing my windpipe. My eyes begin to bulge at the sudden lack of oxygen.

"Solanie, why don't you make this easier for both of us and just do what the fuck I tell you to do!" His voice is terrifying, but his eyes are even scarier.

Even though his face is barely an inch away from mine, his voice sounds so far away. My vision goes blurry and pops of bright light flash all around me. I can see his lips moving, but I can no longer hear anything he's saying. Then, thankfully, everything goes blank.

I awaken to complete silence. It takes a while for my mind to remember my current situation. I cry out as soon as I remember where I'm at and why I'm here.

"Welcome back, Solanie."

That voice.

"I wish you didn't make me do that. You were out for a long time. I was starting to get a lil' worried."

I try to move, but my hands and feet are tied. The room is pitch black, so I can't see how close he is to me. I'm lying on my back, and I'm still naked. My head is throbbing, and the metallic taste of blood is in my mouth.

I hear footsteps across the floor, and then a sudden burst of light brightens up the room. I flinch as my eyes struggle to adjust to the light.

I'm lying on a bed with my hands and feet tied so tightly that I fear the blood circulation will be cut off to both. He sits on the edge of the bed, and it sinks to welcome his weight.

"I'm Deon."

I don't care about his fucking name. "Why are you doing this to me?" I ask him almost immediately.

"Because you're mine, Solanie."

Revulsion ripples through my body, causing me to shudder. Just as I thought, this dude is completely insane.

"I wish you would just listen to what I tell you to do," Deon says as he slides his finger down my face. "Now I have to punish you."

He gets up and cuts the rope that binds my hands and feet. I instantly try to cover my body. He laughs at me, "You don't have to be doing all of that. I've seen your naked body more times than I can count."

Shock hits me first, then repulsion.

"I woulda loved for you to sleep with me here in this bed tonight. But rules are rules, and you gotta suffer the consequence of your disobedience, Solanie." He grabs me by my hair and drags me out of the bed. Even as I fall onto the floor, he doesn't stop pulling me by my hair. It feels like my hair is being ripped straight from my scalp. I struggle to pry his hands away, but Deon is extremely strong and equally as ruthless.

I'm finally granted relief from the burning of my scalp when he releases me to enter a code into the black padlock on the door. I try to get to my feet, but he reaches around my waist and lifts me off the ground. He carries me out of the house. I'm kicking and screaming so loud that my throat feels raw.

"You can scream all ya want. Nobody can hear you. You're thousands of miles from anything!" He laughs at me, looking delirious off the power he has over me.

That can't be true, can it? How long was I knocked out in the trunk of his car? It couldn't have been long enough for him to drive a thousand miles. I realize it doesn't matter if he's telling the truth or not because I'm not going to stop screaming.

I keep screaming until my throat feels like it's about to start bleeding.

The sound of dogs barking forces me to stop screaming, look around, and prepare to defend myself. Ever since I got bitten by a dog when I was a kid, I've had an intense phobia of dogs. I won't even go near a Chihuahua or Shih Tzu.

I frantically look around, trying to find the source of the loud barking.

Deon tosses me to the ground. "Since you don't know how to act, you'll be sleeping with the dogs tonight. They've been trained to obey me, so maybe you can learn a thing or two about obedience from them."

I hear what he's saying, but it takes my mind a minute to comprehend. I'm scrambling to my feet while trying to search for the dogs in the dark of the night. Deon grabs me up in one swoop and leads me closer to the sound of the dogs who sound like they're trying to outbark one another.

He isn't seriously going to force me to sleep with a bunch of viciously barking dogs! I'm on the brink of a breakdown from the continuous onslaught of heightened fear.

"Please," I beg. "Please don't. I'm sorry. I'll do whatever you say!"

Deon stares at me, and his lips curl up into a sick ass smile. "I tried to warn you, Solanie." He opens a chained kennel and tosses me inside, locking the fence behind him.

As soon as I'm thrown into the kennel, two dogs make their way toward me. Even in the dark, I can see that they're big as hell. I jump to my feet, ready to defend myself as best as I can. Their eyes are black, and the closer they come to me, the further I back up until my back is against the tall fence of the kennel.

I toss my eyes over my shoulder and see Deon walking back into the house, not giving a fuck what these dogs do to me.

Two dogs sniff at my feet. I don't know how to interact with them. I've always kept a distance between myself and dogs since that childhood bite. I'm praying that these dogs are friendly despite their intimidating size. I walk to the furthest corner of the kennel and one of the dogs follows me. While the other has lost interest and returns to the other three dogs that are completely indifferent to my presence.

"Shoo!" I wave my hands at the dog, hoping to deter him from getting any closer to me. But the curious mutt won't go away. He walks up to my feet and resumes his sniffing. He doesn't seem aggressive or mean, just inquisitive. I don't drop my guard because that doesn't mean his ass won't snap and bite me at any second. "Shoo! Get away!"

The dog doesn't budge. Instead, he gets closer to me. He sits at my feet, and I release the breath I've been holding. I kneel and pet the top of his furry head. He leans into my petting, and I slowly begin to relax enough to sit next to him.

I'm butt naked sitting in a dog pen with five filthy smelly dogs! The only thing I can do to keep the tears from returning is to laugh. I laugh until my stomach hurts, until I feel like my mind will break.

It's cool out tonight, and the wind is merciless. I ball into a fetal position and the dog lays next to me, offering his fur to me for warmth.

"Good boy," I coo as I continue to pet him. I survey my surroundings. It's dark outside so I can't see much but I can tell I'm in a very wooded area. The kennel I'm locked inside of has to be at least fifteen feet high, making it impossible for any of the dogs to jump over and just as impossible for me to climb over.

I know Deon meant for this sleeping arrangement to be a punishment, but it's really a reward. I'd rather sleep with these dogs any night than be forced to lay next to him and endure God knows what.

Fear, anxiety, and stress have mentally and physically drained me. It's too hard to keep my eyes open. I fall asleep, praying to God that Knight someone finds me and rescues me before

Deon kills me.

FBI SPECIAL AGENT TAYLOR

"You know he's going to beat this thing, right?" Detective Hardee says, and he's actually grinning.

"Fuck you," is all I can say back to him because I don't want to admit he may be right.

I thought I had Kian right where I wanted him, but Kaleb Knight had Kian out before he could even see the judge. I underestimated the pull that the Kings have.

"Well, he is," Detective Hardee continues. "Damn shame too. All that work we put into that sting operation for it to go to shit like that."

"All hope isn't lost," I say, even though I'm having trouble believing it myself.

Detective Hardee shakes his head. "The charges aren't going to stick, Taylor. You saw the way his brother came up in here screaming entrapment."

I cross my arms over my chest. "And? So what?"

Detective Hardee looks at me like I'm the biggest idiot he's ever had a conversation with. "Give it up, Taylor." He pats me on the back and heads toward the door of my office. "Better luck next time."

It takes everything out of me not to throw everything off my desk at the door. Once again, Knight fucking King has me beat.

Most serial killers start to think they're invincible after getting away with as many murders as The Beauty Butcher has. Thinking that way leads to carelessness, and it's that very carelessness that will become The Beauty Butcher's downfall. He's already getting sloppier.

I just got off the phone with our forensic lab who's found some trace evidence recovered from the last crime scene. This is the beginning of the end for The Beauty Butcher.

I race over to the lab and find Mitchell is already there. Lately, he has beat me to every scene. I used to talk shit about Mitchell's work ethic, but he has surprised me with this newfound effort and determination. Our once friendly competition has somehow turned into a rivalry for him. He just wants to be the one to take down The Beauty Butcher. He's chasing the nationwide praise he'll receive for solving such a high-profile case. But I'll be damned if I let him outwork me.

"Late again, Taylor." He has a shit eating grin on his face.

I ignore him and look at the middle-aged forensic scientist, Carol. "What'd you find?"

"Your big break," she answers.

I couldn't have asked for anything better to come out of Carol's mouth. I look over at Mitchell, and he's looking like a man who thinks he'll steal a promotion from me.

Carol pulls up several photos on her computer. She clicks on one and uses a pen to circle the area of the photo she wants us to look at. "You see this? This is a shoe print."

"No way!" I can't believe it. It feels as if we've just hit the police lottery.

Mitchell walks so close up to the computer screen that he

blocks my view. “How did he leave a shoe print? He’s never been that stupid before.”

“I suspect as he was dumping the body, it started to rain. He probably was in a rush to get rid of the body and didn’t expect his shoes to leave imprints in the wet grass.” Carol enlarges the photo of the shoe prints that were taken at the crime scene. “If the body had been found just a few hours later, these prints would have been gone.”

“Wow,” Mitchell says with the shake of his head.

Carol continues, “I’ve analyzed these impressions and compared them to what we have in our database.”

“How does this help us?” Mitchell interrupts. “Those shoes could be old as hell.”

“We have over forty-five thousand shoe tread designs in our database that go back as far as twelve years,” Carol answers. She pulls up another photo. “Get this though. If you compare the photo of this shoe print versus the photo of this one, you can see they’re entirely different.” She pulls up the photos for comparison, and I instantly see what she’s talking about

Mitchell and I gasp at the same time.

“Not only are the styles different, but the sizes are also. So either he had help with the body, or the man we’ve been calling The Beauty Butcher is actually two different men.”

This revelation sends my head reeling, and I feel like I can be knocked over by a feather.

“You’ve got to be shitting me!” Mitchell runs his hand over his head. “Please tell me something else, Carol. Anything but there’s two of these motherfuckers out here.”

“That’s not all.” Carol’s smile is getting bigger. She’s clearly on a roll and proud of her findings. “With these impressions, I was able to determine the brand of shoes our suspects were wearing are Rydes and Nikes.”

"Rydes?" I say.

"Yes, a popular sneaker brand sold at discount stores like Payless and Walmart."

I'm taking notes so fast that my handwriting is sloppy and almost illegible.

"This particular style of Rydes were released fairly recently, which makes our jobs a lot easier. All we have to do is locate all the stores in the Houston area that sell this particular style. Get to those stores and get a hold of their video surveillance, and voila! You'll find your killer." Carol turns and smirks at both of us.

I'm seconds away from kissing this woman.

"Great work, Carol," Mitchell says. He turns to me and says, "Looks like we need to get to work."

I'm more than ready to do just that. Carol has given us more than enough to work with. A lead that will take us straight to The Beauty Butcher.

KNIGHT

I can't stand the sight or smell of pigs inside of my home, but I had to call them. I had to report Solanie's disappearance. I run my hand down my face to calm my rising temper. I know Kurtis and Kian have both of their ears to the streets right now, but I feel like I should be out there. I feel like I'm sitting here wasting time. These cops keep asking me the same questions, re-phrased to sound like a different question.

"How long have you known Miss James?" One of the officers asks me. Not even twenty minutes ago, I was asked the very same thing by one of the other cops.

I sigh and swallow the anger threatening to erupt. "Not long."

"You said you two were dating?"

"Yes."

"This was the first time she'd spent the night here?"

"No."

"Do you believe you could have been followed home, Mr. King?"

"Absolutely not."

"And why is that?"

I try not to smirk. "Because I can tell if someone is following me or not."

"Can you think of anyone who would want to harm you by taking Miss James?"

"Not one."

I answer their repetitive questions, knowing this is leading nowhere. I can tell they don't really want to help a nigga. I'm the same man they've been working so hard to arrest. They probably think I killed Solanie or some shit, and I'm only trying to cover it up with a false missing person's report.

I look over at the two detectives who are going through my tampered surveillance system. I know they're not looking for clues that can help find Solanie, but for evidence they can use against me in whatever case they've been building. Little do they know, anything that could remotely look incriminating has long been deleted before they brought their asses here.

"We have someone at Miss James' mother's house now breaking the news to her family."

I feel the weight of guilt fall heavy on me. I've never met Solanie's mother, and now her first impression of me will be the fact I let somebody snatch her daughter from my front door.

I just don't believe there could ever be anyone that crazy to harm Solanie in order to get to me. If anything, she should have been safe because of me.

Finally, after too many hours, the police pack up their shit and leave my home. I immediately hop in my car and head to my father's office where he's finishing up a meeting with Rax, this African nigga that can hack into the CIA's computer system if he wanted to.

"'Sup, my brother." He stands up to greet me when I enter the room.

"Hey, Rax. How you doing?"

"Better than you, I have to assume."

I want to knock the shit out of Rax, but I know it's in his culture to say exactly what's on his mind with no filter.

"Knight, Rax is here to help us," Kurtis tells me as if I don't already know that shit by him sitting here.

"I'm gunna check everything out on Solanie," Rax says, and he butchers the pronunciation of Solanie's name.

So-lawn-e muthafucka, I want to correct his ass, but it doesn't really matter at this point.

"Everything like what?" I say.

Kurtis asks me, "You still have her cell?"

I hand Rax the cell phone Solanie had gone outside to get the night she was abducted.

"I'm gunna match every number she's been in contact with these last couple of months to a name and an address. I'll trace all da missed calls and text messages, even da deleted ones."

I don't doubt Rax can do any of this. He's the best at what he does, and that's why he's sitting in Kurtis' office right now.

"I want a copy of those texts," I tell Rax.

"Of course," he says, his accent thick as maple syrup. "Can you make me a list of her friends and family? I will get my team to run a check on all of 'em. You never know. They could be involved somehow."

I can't argue with Rax. I should have done a better job at checking out the people connected to Solanie. I was in too big of a hurry trying to get to know her that I didn't do what needed to be done. Before anyone enters our lives, a thorough check has to be done on not only them, but everyone connected to them. Being a King, we have to be suspicious of everyone.

"Is it possible that this could all be a set up?" Rax asks.

"What the fuck is that supposed to mean?" I'm two seconds from whooping this nigga's ass all the way back to Africa.

"The girl," he answers calmly. "Could she have orchestrated all of this in an attempt to get to your family? Like a ransom or something?"

I don't want to think about that even being a possibility. And by the way Kurtis is staring at me, I can tell that better *not* be a possibility.

I haven't known Solanie for that long, but I know she isn't built like that. She isn't one of those money grubbing hoodrats out looking for the next big paycheck. She didn't even know who I was when she met me. I'm a good judge of character, and my instincts have never lead me wrong, so I am fully persuaded it's true when I say, "Naw. Solanie ain't like that."

Rax stands up. He shakes Kurtis's hand and then mine before he walks to the door. "I'll be in touch."

I nod and return my eyes to my father. I'm now noticing that Kian isn't here. He should have been present for a meeting like this. "Where's Kian?"

Kurtis shakes his head. "He said he was working on some kinda leads. If you ask me, he's enjoying this a little too much. You know he just needs a reason."

I don't have time for Kian's bullshit right now, but I know better than to leave him to his own devices. Without Kurtis saying another word, I know what I need to do. I have to find my knuckle-head ass little brother before he makes a bad situation a lot worse.

DEON

I have to break her.

She isn't the Solanie I first laid eyes on. That sadness that attracted me to her has evaporated and been replaced with a self-confidence that I can't stand. She's now no different than all the other bitches out there that walk around like they're God's gift to a nigga. The ones who look straight past me like I'm not even worth a glance.

Now, I have to show Solanie this is her new reality, and there is nothing she can do but accept it. The quicker she accepts that, the easier things will be for *both* of us.

I watch her curl into the fetal position in the corner of the kennel. Gumbo, my German Shepard mix, is huddled up close to her. The corners of my mouth rise into a smile. Gumbo has already taken a liking to her. There's just something about that fucking Solanie that draws everything to her like a magnet.

Staring at her sleeping in the dog pen gives me an idea I hadn't thought of before. Solanie has a lot more fight in her than I'd expected. She won't be easily broken, so I'm going to have to train her like I've done my dogs. I'll take away everything that gives her the strength to fight me. I'll strip away every piece of her dignity and reduce her to nothing until she's just as trained as one of my dogs. The way she glares at me with hatred and disgust will soon turn to gratefulness and love. She'll learn to look forward to the times that I come home and run up to me like the dogs do every time I enter their kennel.

It's genius. I can't believe I didn't think of it before now.

I unlock the kennel. Solanie jumps up. Horror contorts her beautiful facial features, and I laugh because her fear feels good to me. I feed off it like it's a five-star meal.

I pretend to ignore her as I feed my dogs, each of them eager for their first meals but proficiently trained to sit and wait until I give the command for them to eat.

Gumbo abandons Solanie and joins the rest of the pack, ready to be fed. I take my time filling their bowls with food and fresh water. I release them to eat and slowly walk up to Solanie. She's defiant. She refuses to look at me. Such a difficult girl.

"Good morning, Solanie."

Her bottom lip trembles. She still refuses to look at me.

I know how to get her right though. It'll be no different than how I trained each dog she shared this kennel with last night.

"Stand up." I make sure to put enough force in my voice to let her know that I'm not fucking around.

She's trembling, but she obeys and stands up. I let my eyes roam the naked body that now belongs to me. She's filthy and smells like a dog. She has dried mud all over her feet and knees.

I grab her by the back of her neck, and she yelps. My grip is tight and unrelenting. I lead her out of the kennel. The door automatically closes and locks behind us. Solanie is full of questions now. Where am I taking her? What am I going to do to her? Am I going to kill her?

I ignore all her questions and take her to the basement of the house. This will be her new home until she learns how to obey. I throw her inside, and she falls to the floor. I grab her right ankle and lock it into a chamber that's connected to a pole in the center of the room. Now, she won't be able to move but five feet, if that. The chain attached to the shackle wallops loudly every time she moves.

"Please!" She cries out as soon as she realizes she's trapped. I watch in satisfaction as her face goes through a series of emotions. Shock, confusion, fear, and finally defeat.

"You smell like dog shit," I let her know.

She's crying and burying her face in her dirty ass hands. Her shoulders shake with every sob.

Her tears and agony turn me the fuck on, and I savor her grief and fear like a crème brûlée. My dick is so hard it's straining against my jeans trying to escape. I planned on waiting, but all my self-control don't mean shit when I'm looking at Solanine naked *and* crying.

I walk up to her and yank her head upwards by grabbing a fistful of her hair. Damn, she's so beautiful when she's scared. I use my other hand to unzip my jeans and free my throbbing dick. She gasps, and I can't tell if it's out of fear of what I'm about to do or in shock of my size. I choose to believe the latter.

I shove myself in her face, but her lips don't budge. "Open your fuckin' mouth," I growl.

She's crying harder, but her lips still don't open, as if they've been stapled together. I tighten my grip on her head, ready to slam her face onto the concrete floor of this basement if that's what it's going to take to make her open her pretty little mouth.

The sound of loud knocking makes me almost jump out of my skin. Absolutely nobody knows about this house. Plus, it's in the middle of nowhere. I release Solanie and stuff my dick back into my jeans before leaving the basement. I grab my gun, check to make sure it's loaded, and slowly inch toward the front door.

It's absolutely impossible for the cops to have tracked Solanie here. So, my mind instantly goes to Knight before ruling him out just as quickly. Still, as I walk to the door, my hand is on the trigger. I ain't taking no chances.

The knocking gets louder and antagonizes the beating of my heart.

Now, I wish I had installed a peephole on the door, some windows, or something that would allow me to see who's on the other side now. I cock my gun, take a deep breath, and slowly open the door.

SOLANIE

I cry until the tears stop coming, until my throat is raw and burning. I cry as if crying will get me out of this place. No matter how loud I scream or how hard I plead, I know my appeals are falling on deaf ears. Deon was right; no one can hear me. I'm trapped, and now I'm running low on faith.

I look around the room Deon locked me in. It's bare except for the metal pole that I'm attached to that reaches all the way to the ceiling of the room. I can stand up, but the chain prevents me from walking anywhere near the door that Deon walked out of.

There's no bathroom in here. As if that even matters. Last night, I was forced to relieve myself just like the dogs that I slept with. I'll probably have to do the same here.

I smell horrible and feel just as bad. My energy level is low because I haven't eaten in so long. My mouth feels as if I've stuffed hundreds of cotton balls inside of it. I lick my dry cracked lips, but my tongue is just as dry. I wonder if Deon plans on leaving me down in this room to die of dehydration.

Thoughts race one another in my head, thoughts of escape and overpowering Deon, though that'll be damn near impossible. That dude is freakishly strong, and the high levels of fear my body has had to endure all night has made me too weak to put up any kind of real fight against Deon.

I feel hopeless.

What's the point of fighting a losing battle? Physically, I'm no match for Deon. I can't escape, and I have no other options.

I bring my knees to my chest and try not to think about the things Deon is going to do to me. I can tell by the crazy ass look in his eyes that he's not right in the head. If that loud knocking hadn't stopped him... I don't even want to think about what would have happened! A whole new wave of fear washes over me because I know when that time comes again, there will be nothing I can do to stop him.

My mind goes to the months of my life that were wasted in depression. The days that I even considered suicide, thinking there was no way I could live without Myron. Now that I'm so close to death, I realize I do *not* want to die. I was foolish for ever thinking life wasn't worth living just because some nigga walked away from me.

I want to live! I want to see my momma again. I want to laugh with my girls again. I want to see Knight again...

I start to pray because even though I feel helpless, I know that God has the power to help me. I pray until a resilient desire to *fight* replaces all hopelessness. I will *not* go down easily. I think about my daddy and know he wouldn't want me to just give up so readily. I'm stronger than that.

Why hadn't I been more careful, more aware of my surroundings? Maybe then I would have noticed this nigga hiding somewhere in the shadows, waiting for the right moment to snatch me up. In a million scenarios, I would have never thought something like this could happen to me, especially not outside of Knight's house. Not the man everyone seems to be so afraid of, the man who seems to be the unofficial mayor of the city.

Deon obviously doesn't give a fuck about Knight or who he's connected to. He was completely fearless when he took Knight's girl straight from his front door.

Knight's girl.

Yesterday, when I said that, a million feel-good chills ran down my body. Now, I don't feel shit.

Disappointment has replaced every emotion I thought I felt for Knight. I'm disappointed that I allowed myself to be dis-illusioned into thinking Knight could somehow find and rescue me. This isn't some fairytale bullshit; this is real.

And in real life, sometimes the bad guys win.

DEON

I'm fully prepared to shoot whoever is on the other side of this door. I swing it open with one hand while my finger is on the trigger of my gun in my other hand.

Nate.

He doesn't even react to the gun that's pointed directly in his face. I'm surprised to see him here, but I shouldn't be. He pushes past me into the house. He's angry. No, he's way past that. He's pissed the fuck off.

"What the hell is wrong with you?" I want to know.

He ignores me and goes straight to the TV. He turns it on, fiddles with the antenna, then flips through the channels until he finds what he's looking for. He turns the volume up loud and glares at me as the news anchor delivers breaking news.

"Police now have evidence that the serial killer known as The Beauty Butcher is not just one man as what was previously suspected."

I stumble backwards a few feet. How the fuck...?

We've never left a witness alive to reveal that. I look to Nate for answers, but his eyes are cemented to the TV.

"The Houston Police Department have joined forces with the FBI in order to track these dangerous killers. Law enforcement believes with this latest development, they're making substantial progress in the case. Police have not released many details, but we now know that major evidence was recovered from the last victim's crime scene. Police believe that evidence, coupled with the newfound revelation of there being two killers, will soon lead to an arrest." The anchor looks relieved to be delivering all these bombshells. I, on the other hand, feel like I'm about to pass the hell out.

I don't even want to look at Nate. We've always been so careful, never left any kind of evidence in the past, so how the hell could the police now have evidence?

"We fucked up, Deon," Nate sounds troubled. I've never seen my brother afraid of anything, so I know this is real bad. "This is on every fuckin' channel!" He flips through the channels until he finds another news station delivering the same breaking news on The Beauty Butcher.

Even though the police don't know anything about our identities, they now know that there's two of us, and to Nate, that's just as bad.

I collapse on the couch and bury my face into my hands. I feel like the room is starting to close in on me. I need to think, but I can't with Nate pacing back and forth screaming how we're going to get the chair for all we've done.

I have to somehow fix this. I can't let the cops close in on us. I interrupt Nate's tirade by saying, "But they don't really know shit, do they?"

"You tell me, Deon! How is it possible *we* left evidence at this scene when we've never done so before?"

I knew this was coming. I knew he was going to try to blame this on me. I try to think back to that day, but it's a haze. That night he tried to warn me, but I wouldn't listen. Usually, I'd know beforehand the spot to dump the body, somewhere in obscurity where it'd take the police weeks to find. This last time though, I didn't feel like searching high and low. I was too anxious to get back to Solanie. To make sure she wasn't spending too much time with Knight. It was late and raining, so I just picked anywhere. It wasn't planned, and when you do shit off the rift like that, you're bound to fuck up. Lesson number one from Daddy.

I shake my head back and forth so hard it almost hurts. "I know we couldn't have left evidence at the scene!"

"Did you not just watch the same shit that I did!" Nate is glaring at me. "I told you we shouldn't have dumped that bitch's body there. It was too in the open. Too much traffic on that part of town!"

Why didn't I listen? Now I gotta worry about some kind of evidence leading back to Nate and me. I look at Nate. Yeah, he's pissed off, but I know better. He'd be a lot more enraged if the cops knew more than what the news is saying. If they had something bigger, Nate would know.

"What do we do now?" I ask him.

"*We* don't do anything," he sneers at me. "You're gonna keep your ass right here and out of trouble." He stops glaring at me and starts back pacing. He stops abruptly as if a thought just tasered him. "Did you destroy everything you were wearing that night?"

I nod. I always do.

He lets out a breath of relief. "Stay here until all this shit blows over. I won't be able to do anything for a while now that everything is so hot," he says with frustration.

That's why he's really mad. Yeah, he's upset that the police have some kind of evidence now, but he's more upset that whatever evidence they have has made it too hot for him to do any hunting. I feel bad for him, and I'm even that much gladder that I have Solanie. My hunting days are over. For all I care, Nate can be The Beauty Butcher all by his damn self now.

"So where is she?" Nate says as if he can see straight through my thoughts. "Where's your lil' toy?"

I'm smiling before I can even stop myself. I get up, and Nate follows me down the stairs into the basement. Solanie instantly jumps up at the sound of the door opening. Her eyes go wide when she notices Nate beside me. I know she's afraid to see that I have someone with me, but she doesn't have to worry. Nate knows better than to touch what's mine.

Nate takes his time looking Solanie over, but his facial expression doesn't change. "Even after seeing her in person, I still don't know why you're so fascinated with her."

The insult stings, but I don't show it. Nate is just jealous that I found Solanie first and claimed her.

He walks up closer to her, and Solanie flinches as if he's hit her.

"Have you heard of The Beauty Butcher?" he asks her.

Solanie doesn't answer him. She just stares at him.

Nate chuckles, and a sinister smile creeps onto his face. "Do you realize my little brother over there *is* The Beauty Butcher?"

Solanie's face goes aghast. She looks past Nate and directly at me. Her bottom lip starts quivering, and I can smell the fear seeping from her pores. She's probably thinking back to all the news coverage she's watched over the months about The Beauty Butcher. She's probably freaking out realizing she's his next victim.

But Solanie doesn't even realize what my brother has just done. I know exactly why he told Solanie that I'm The Beauty Butcher. He knows the feelings that I have for her. That I've been contemplating not killing her and just keeping her here with me.

By revealing I'm The Beauty Butcher to Solanie, Nate is ensuring that she won't ever leave this house alive to tell anyone.

SOLANIE

It hurts to even open my eyes. My head is throbbing, and my mind feels like it's turning to mush. I don't know how long I've been here, but it feels like a very long time.

Deon brought me a bottle of water some time ago, and I haven't seen him since. I want to say it's only been a few hours, but with no way to tell day from night, it could have been weeks.

If I would have known he was going to be gone for so long, I wouldn't have devoured the bottle of water as quickly as I did. Now, my mouth is so dry I can't even open it. I don't know what dehydration feels like, but I think I'm about to die of it. I'm also so hungry that it hurts. Maybe it would be better if I just gave up and died right here...

When I hear the door open, I try to open my eyes, but even that is too hard to do. I know it's Deon anyway. The Beauty Butcher...

"Solanie." He sings my name. "Are you hungry?"

I try to open my mouth to answer him, but I swear it feels like my mouth has been glued shut. He knows the answer anyway.

He walks up to me and brings a bottle of water to my lips. The moisture against my cracked lips feels like heaven. I finally open my mouth and greedily gulp down the cold water.

"Thirsty girl," Deon says with amusement.

I hate the sound of his voice.

He pulls the bottle of water away, and I start to protest

until I smell the aroma of food. I see he's holding a greasy white fast-food bag, and my stomach lurches, demanding the unhealthy sustenance.

"I betchu hungry. It's been about three days since you had something to eat."

Three days! I would scream if I had the strength to do so.

Deon waves the bag of food in front of me as if it were a bone and I'm a starving dog. He's relishing in the fact that he has something I desperately need.

"So this is how this shit is gonna work," he says slowly. "You need to eat, or you'll probably die. I'll feed you, but only if you obey."

I'm not in the position to argue with this maniac, so I don't say anything.

"First thing's first; you need a bath."

I do smell horrible, but the only thing I care about right now is whatever is in that greasy bag he's holding on to.

"Are you going to be a good girl and let me bathe you?"

My stomach turns at the thought of Deon touching me, but it's also growling, so I nod.

"I don't know what that means, Solanie. I asked you a question. I expect an answer."

"Y-yes."

The biggest grin I've ever seen appears on his ugly ass face. He drops the bag where he knows is out of my reach and then walks out of the room.

The smell of the food that I can't reach is like torture to my starving body. For the first time ever, I'm grateful to see Deon when he returns to the room. He's carrying a bucket and a purple sponge, and excitement is dancing in his eyes.

He sits next to me and dips the sponge into the water. "Sit

up," he instructs me.

I obey without hesitation. He smiles at this and reaches inside the paper bag. When his hand comes out, it's full of French fries. He gives them to me, and I devour them like a rabid animal.

"See, Solanie. When you obey, you get rewarded." He brings the sponge up to the back of my neck and the warm soapy water runs down my back. I hate that the warmth of the water feels so good.

Deon rubs my neck and back. He dips the sponge back into the water and starts on my collarbone. The water tickles as it drips onto my breasts and stomach. Deon's eyes are ravenous, and I hate that he's touching me, but I know I can't protest. Not when I'm this close to getting food.

It's like Deon can read my mind because he drops the sponge into the bucket, dries his hands on his shirt and reaches back into the fast-food bag. He pulls out two chicken nuggets and I snatch them from him.

He finds this amusing and starts laughing. I barely chew the nuggets and look to him with eyes begging for more.

"Stand up."

It takes longer than it should, but I manage to stand. The hunger pangs seem to be getting stronger now that I've had a tiny amount of food.

Deon spreads my legs and the shackle on my ankle screeches loudly. He runs the sponge down my stomach and the water races down my thighs. I flinch when he presses the sponge in between my legs. He licks his lips. I hate him.

Up and down. Down and up. The sponge runs across my thighs and legs. Over my feet and then he's rubbing the sponge on my back and butt. He spreads my butt cheeks and I feel the sponge touching me in places I don't want Deon to even see.

I gasp when I feel his fingers touch the lips of my vagina. I want to pull away from his touch, but I fear he'll withhold the food if I do so.

He spends too much time washing between my legs, showing me he can touch me wherever he wants, and there's not a damn thing I can do about it. When he finally moves his hand and sponge, I release the breath I was holding. He finishes washing me to his satisfaction and then dries my body. I'm shivering, even though it's so hot down here.

"Good girl," Deon says.

He tosses me the bag, and I dive into it as if it's my last meal. I probably shouldn't eat all of it because I'm not sure when Deon will feed me again, but the hunger demands me to devour everything in the bag.

Deon leaves, and I'm glad that I'm able to at least enjoy the food without him gawking at me. That doesn't last long though because he's back before I even finish the cheeseburger. His hands are now gloved, and he's carrying a mop and another bucket. I turn my head when I see he's cleaning up my waste.

It's so dehumanizing to have to squat to shit and piss in the corner of the room like a damn dog, but it feels even worse having Deon clean up after me. I'm ashamed, and I don't want to watch him do it.

By the time I finish eating, Deon is done cleaning the room. It now smells like Pine Sol. He leaves again without saying anything to me. I'm grateful to no longer be hungry, to be cleaned and also in a fresh smelling room. It's crazy how Deon managed to make me grateful to him for these bare necessities. I absolutely hate him for it.

The door opens, and he's back. He sits a bucket next to me. "It's time to housebreak you."

My face goes hot with shame.

"You will use the restroom in that bucket from now on." He

throws a t-shirt at me. "Here."

I look at him with appreciative eyes. I can't believe how happy a t-shirt has made me. I quickly put it on, feeling a little of my dignity return now that I'm no longer forced to be naked in front of him.

Deon is smiling, devouring all of my gratefulness. "Keep obeying, and you'll keep being rewarded."

He gives me a look that freezes me in place. I know the next time he comes to see me, he's going to want to do more than bathe me. I'm also ashamed to admit that I'll more than likely obey him in exchange for food and water.

Like a good little dog.

FBI SPECIAL AGENT TAYLOR

The Special Task Force hit the ground running. In less than forty-eight hours, our department was able to compile a list of stores in the area that carry the Rydes shoes that match the imprint from the crime scene. Now everyone is running around trying to put the puzzle pieces together, especially Mitchell, who was somehow able to get himself named head of the unit responsible for going through the endless hours of store surveillance video.

I grab my ringing cell, and I'm surprised to see it's Detective Hardee.

"Detective," I answer. "This is a surprise hearing from you."

"You're a hard woman to reach," he says.

"Damn Butcher case has been keeping me busy."

"I heard you guys are really making progress on that thing."

Pride threatens to erupt into a large smile on my face, but I don't let it. "Yeah. It won't be long before it's a closed case. Anyway, what's up?"

"I've left you like four messages. I knew you didn't get them when you didn't call me back. You won't believe this!"

My palm starts itching with excitement. I know whatever

is about to come out of Detective Hardee's mouth is going to be good.

"Knight's girlfriend was abducted from his home a few days ago."

"Shut up!" I slap my hand across my desk. My mouth hangs open. He's right; I can't believe this.

"Yes, ma'am. Whoever did it must have a vendetta against him because get this. They took the time to hack into his surveillance system and erase everything."

"No shit?"

"None at all. You should have seen the bastard. He looked like he wanted to go on a murder rampage."

"Shit." I bit my lip as a thousand scenarios run through my head. "Do you think this is real? I mean, this is Knight King that we're talking about. He could have killed the girl and made up all this abduction stuff to cover his tracks."

Detective Hardee doesn't sound convinced. "No way. You didn't see this guy's face. This is definitely real. What worries me though is him finding who's responsible before we do."

That's a good point. If Knight finds the culprit before the police, we'll be none the wiser, and their body parts will probably be spread out all across the city.

"Who in their right mind would fuck with Knight like this?" I think aloud.

"Your guess is as good as mine," the detective says.

My mind is on overdrive trying to see how I can use this abduction to the advantage of my case against Knight. I know Knight should be the last thing on my mind right now, but this is too good to ignore. He has to be stressed out of his mind right now. That stress will cause him not to be able to think as quickly on his feet. Which means now is the time for me to pay Knight a visit.

"I'm thinking this has drug activity all over it," Detective Hardee says. "Maybe the girl was abducted to settle a score...?"

"No way that it's a local dealer. No one in the city is that bold," I say.

"Mexican cartel?"

"Possible but not likely," I say. "I don't think the Kings are affiliated with any cartels."

"Hell, for all we know, she could be the unlucky victim of The Beauty Butchers," Hardee says playfully.

I grimace. As much as I can't stand Knight, I wouldn't wish that on my worst enemy.

"Speaking of the Butcher case, a lady came down to the precinct awhile back saying she has some kind of information that she thinks could be related to the case. Lady looked and sounded like a crack pot, but one of our officers took her statement anyway. It's probably a waste of time, but I have her contact info if you want it."

I grab a pad and take down the woman's name and number. It could very well be a dead end, but it's still worth checking out. I end the call with Hardee and call the woman, Chandie Tocks, immediately.

"It's about time somebody got back with me," she says after I've introduced myself to her. "I know who's out here cutting bitches faces and shit, and y'all acting like y'all don't even want the information."

"I'm sorry it's taken this long for someone to reach out to you," I say. "Can you elaborate on what you've just stated?"

"Do you remember the case of a Rochelle Jamison?"

"Not off the top of my head," I answer as I quickly type the name into my computer. It's an eighteen-year-old cold murder case of a runaway turned prostitute. She'd been brutally raped and murdered, body dumped at a truck stop. There were never any suspects or persons of interest.

"What does her case have to do with The Beauty Butchers?" I ask.

Chandie sighs like I'm starting to get on her nerves. "She was killed the same way the Butchers are killing women now!"

I click through the case files and sure enough, the victim's facial injuries are eerily similar to The Butcher's work.

"Do you mind if we meet in person?" I ask Chandie.

"You gonna have to come to me because I done already came down there once and wasted my time 'cause y'all didn't take me serious."

I grab my jacket and car keys. "Where are you located, Miss Tocks? I can be there in less than an hour."

I hang up after I've gotten her address. I'm not sure if these cases are in any way linked, but I'm not going to rule it out until I have more details. I hop into my car on a new mission.

But first, I'm going to make a pit stop by Knight's pill mill.

KNIGHT

The whole world is going on around me as if nothing is different. People are living their lives going about their business as if a catastrophe hasn't just hit the city.

Even my clinic is still doing business as usual with a line around the block. As soon as I walk through the door, I know I'm going to be closing up early. I'm not in the mood to be here surrounded by pill heads, no matter how much they're paying per prescription.

I slam the door to my office and sit behind my desk. I bury my face in my hands and demand myself to think straight. It's a hard thing to do when rage is taking up so much space in my brain.

"What!" I boom at the sound of a knock on my door. Whoever is daring to interrupt my silence will get the brunt of my anger.

"Damn, nigga!" Kian walks through the door. His voice is playful, but his face is serious. "You alright?"

"No, Kian. I'm not alright," I sneer.

He sits across from me, and I can tell he's trying to measure his words. "Damn, bro. I know you fucked up right now, but you gotta keep ya cool."

I tilt my head at the irony of Kian of all people telling me I need to keep my cool. If everything wasn't so fucked up right now, this would be comical.

"You know that fool Rax is on his way over here."

This makes me look up. “Word? The nigga ain’t called me.”

“Pops just told me. He on his way, too,” Kian says.

Rax must have found something big for Kurtis to be driving all the way over here. I’m kind of mad that Rax didn’t notify me first, but I know he has to follow the chain of command.

“I don’t think no hood niggas had anything to do with this,” Kian says. He pulls his cell phone out and starts texting someone. “I done talked to everybody, and nobody knows shit.”

I figured as much.

I stare at my knuckles as Kian starts rambling on and on about his baby momma drama bullshit. I know he’s trying to take my mind off Solanie, but he’s going about it the wrong way if he thinks I give a fuck about Alexis’ latest antics.

Finally, Kurtis and Rax arrive. We sit around my desk, and I brush past the formalities, ravenous for whatever Rax has found out. It’s been five days since Solanie went missing. I know the statistics, and it’s unlikely that she’s even still alive at this point.

Rax pulls out a folder. He slowly pulls out a few pieces of paper. He seems to be moving in slow motion by how slow he’s taking his time getting to the point.

“This Solanie is very clean,” he says in accented English. He hands me a piece of paper that contains several text messages that Solanie exchanged with her mother and friends.

I scan through them and when I see my name mentioned, a smile inches onto my face. I read her texts with Mariah about how much she was feeling me, and my chest starts to swell.

“As you can see from all these messages, she wasn’t involved with any other men or nothin’ like that,” Rax says. “Most of her messages are about regular things.

I already knew that, but I’m glad Kurtis heard it for himself. I know he was thinking that I'd messed up and somehow misjudged Solanie's character.

"Her parents?" Kurtis asks.

"Straight as line," Rax says.

"What the fuck then?" Kian blurts out.

"I did a little digging and looked into the IP addresses of visitors to Solanie's social media pages."

"And?" I exclaim. I need Rax to shoot straight to the point.

He slides a piece of paper toward me with a number on it that means nothing to me.

"What's an IP address?" Kian asks him.

"It's a number that identifies each computer using the Internet Protocol to communicate over a network," Rax explains.

"Layman's terms please," Kurtis says.

"It's a way we can find the general location of tha muthafuckas that went on Solanie's pages. And that one right there was on her page the most," Rax says as he points to the number on the paper.

I reach for the paper again, but I don't see how the numbers tell me where anybody lives.

Rax explains, "That IP address is for a location in Katy."

"Give it to me," I immediately demand.

"I'm working on getting the exact location. Right now, all I know is someone in Katy was very interested in Solanie. I was also able to link that same IP address to this Facebook and SnapChat account." He slides another piece of paper to me.

I'm looking at the photo of a blonde-haired white girl. I look up at Rax. "I ain't never seen this bitch before."

Rax nods. "More likely than not, it's a fake account. Whoever kept going on Solanie's page set up those fake accounts so they could see things she only shares with those following her."

"So what does all this mean, Rax?" Kurtis asks.

"Someone was stalking Solanie," he answers flatly.

"The fuck?" I hear myself saying aloud.

Kian laughs, but it's not a *ha-ha that's funny* laugh. It's a murderous and full of anticipation of doing something deadly laugh.

"If someone was stalking Solanie, they've more than likely been inside her place, stole some shit and left some trace of themselves there and so on. Can you get me access to her place? I need to get in there and take a look around," Rax says.

"I don't have a key to her place," I admit. "Plus, the cops have already been all through her shit. Whatever you looking for, they probably already found."

Rax shakes his head. "Not if they don't know what they're looking for."

Kurtis rubs his chin, and I can almost see the wheels spinning in his head. "We can get you access, Rax. How soon can you get there?"

"As soon as you say the word."

I jot down Solanie's address and hand it to Rax.

Some of the apprehension I walked in here with has melted away. I feel like we're making progress. I know for sure we know more than the police know. They're sitting somewhere with their thumbs up their asses, worried about me instead of looking for whoever took Solanie.

Someone was stalking her? I have a hunger for revenge that won't be satiated until my bare hands are wrapped around the throat of whoever fucked with what's mine.

"I'll be in touch." Rax stands and walks toward the door.

When he opens it, Reece, the clinic's front desk receptionist, is standing there looking all flustered and out of breath.

"I tried to stop her!" Reese says as a tall, thin woman charges past her and enters my office.

Kurtis, Kian, and Rax look at the woman before turning to look at me. I shrug.

The woman has a smug look on her face, and even though she's in plain clothes, I already know that she's a cop. She looks too young to be a detective, but that doesn't mean she isn't one. Her hair is slicked back into a short ponytail. She has delicate feminine features, but there's something very masculine about the way she's sizing everybody up in the room right now.

"Well, don't you all leave on my account," she says. Her voice and facial expression is condescending as hell.

"Who are you?" I ask. "And what the fuck are you doing back here? If you tryin' to see a doctor, you gonna have to wait in line like everybody else." I look her up and down like she's trash.

I get the reaction I want out of her when offense washes over her face. She plays it off quickly though. "I'm Special Agent Taylor with the FBI, and I need to ask you a few questions, Mr. King."

Kurtis gives me a look that only I would be able to understand. I sit back down and fold my hands across my desk. My demeanor goes lax, and arrogance laces my voice. "Alright, Agent Taylor. Have a seat."

DEON

Solanie is a fast learner. It's amazing what a little hunger and thirst will make a person do. There's a method to my madness with her. I locked her away for three days with only a bottle of water to sustain her. It wasn't my fault she didn't properly ration the water and drunk it all the first day. By day three, she was willing to do anything for a burger and bottle of water.

I could have taken that pussy then, but there's a pace that I have to take this training. When she allowed me to bathe her without resistance, I knew she was on the verge of breaking. I almost broke my damn self when I had my hands all on her body. I've been fantasizing about touching her for so long that when it was finally happening, I almost bust inside my jeans.

I'm a man of self-control, so I was able to get a hold of myself. I bathed her, fed her, and left her. Even though I have an unusually high degree of self-control, I wasn't able to limit the raging desire for a sexual release. Instead of getting on Swipe or Like, I jacked off to the memory of how Solanie's skin felt. I don't think I've ever busted a nut that powerful before, and it was in my own damn hands. So I can only imagine how it's going to feel when I'm finally inside of Solanie.

Now that she's mine.

I managed to stay away for three days, but now that I'm back, the anticipation of seeing her again is suffocating.

As soon as I enter the basement, she sits upright. She's looking at me with eyes of expectancy. She's happy to see me. I knew eventually she would be. She's been here hungry and lonely, with nothing but her own thoughts. Of course, she's excited to see me, *her master*.

If she wasn't tied to that pole, she'd run up to me and jump all over me like a dog happy to be reunited with its owner.

"I thought you'd never come back," she says. Her voice is hoarse with thirst. I look at the empty water bottle next to her and wonder how long it lasted her this time.

I also notice the smell of human waste, but I don't see any. Which means she used the bucket as I instructed. I set the bag of food down out of her reach, put a pair of latex gloves on and grab her waste bucket which is almost full. I'm not repulsed by it, because it's something Solanie produced. I leave to empty it.

When I return, Solanie's eyes are wide and begging. She's never been more beautiful to me.

I sit on the stool that I brought with me and take my time opening the to-go box full of barbecue ribs, brisket, roasted corn, and potato salad. I would have gone with a less fattening meal, but Solanie is already starting to get too thin for my tastes.

Her eyes go wet as she watches me eat a piece of the rib. I know her head is on the brink of insanity having been here alone for so long with only hunger to keep her company.

"It's bath time," I tell her after I swallow the deliciously seasoned rib.

She nods her head so hard that she looks like a bobble head toy.

I laugh at my little Solanie, so eager to please me.

I start bathing her, but I can't take my time this time. I want to get this bath over with so that I can bury myself inside of her.

After her bath, I hand her the food and reprimand her for eating so fast. I watch her eat the food as if she won't get another meal and decide I won't have her go without food for so long anymore.

"How long have I been here?" she surprises me by asking.

"Uh, about six days or so."

Her eyes widen, but she doesn't say anything. She sucks on the rib bone in a way that strains my self-control.

"My mom…? Is she okay?"

I shift in the chair. I don't like the direction this conversation is going. Why is she worried about anybody from her past? She's never going to see any of them again.

"Don't ask me shit about nobody from ya old life," I tell her. Something is telling me she doesn't really care about her mom. It's Knight who she really wants to ask about. I can't stop my fury as I bring my foot down on her. If she won't willingly forget about Knight, I'll just have to beat his memory out of her.

I'm the wrong nigga for her to try like this. She was doing so good up until now. She cowers away from my kicks and cries out for me to stop. I manage to get a hold on my anger, and she crawls as far away from me as she can get. Which isn't far since her ankle is still chained to that pole.

She doesn't ask any more questions after that, so I decide she deserves a reward for her obedience. I dig in my bag and hand her a dress I'd taken from her closet a long time ago.

As soon as she sees it, she sits up. Her mouth opens, and tears start falling down her face.

"What's wrong? You don't wanna wear it?"

Her sobs don't stop but she nods. "I do want to wear it. It's just… it feels good to see something from my…"

Past.

She doesn't have to say it for me to know what she *wants* to say. She grips her side as if she's preparing to be kicked again. I decide to let her make it this time.

She reaches for the bottle of water and takes two small gulps before placing the top back on it. She's measuring how much to drink because she doesn't know when she'll be given another bottle.

I'm tripping out on how fast she learns.

I pull a gallon jug of water from my bag and Solanie gasps. Her cries are replaced by several repeated thanks to me. I hadn't expected her to voice her gratitude in this way, and I can't withhold the monster inside of me any longer.

My right hand stretches out to clutch one of her breasts, and she gasps. She recoils at first, but then her body goes rigidly still. She knows better than to fight me.

Good girl.

I take her nipple in my mouth and suck it like a man dying of thirst. So many times, I dreamed about this moment, but it's more satisfying than any wet dream I ever had.

"Lay back," I demand. I should be gentle with her, but I can't.

I won't.

She obeys me, and I know I won't be able to last long. "Spread your legs."

She does as she's told, and I ignore the fact that her eyes are shut tight. I ignore the heaving of her chest. She wants this as much as I do. That's why she isn't fighting That's why she's obeying me so well. I look at her beautiful pussy and growl like the animal I am.

She doesn't shut her legs. She doesn't react to my animalistic growls. She simply does as I say.

Good girl.

SOLANIE

I knew this was going to happen sooner or later. All the hours I've been locked in here, I tried to mentally prepare for this very moment. But no amount of mental preparation could ever make me ready for something as terrible as this. I try not to cry, but I can feel my heart literally breaking inside of my chest.

I lay as still as possible as he violates me in the worst way. I refuse to open my eyes because I know the image of him on top of me will forever haunt me. I silently sob, wondering how I'll ever be able to recover from this.

He keeps saying my name along with a lot of other nonsensical things about how much he loves me and how I belong to him.

I don't know how or when, but I will make it out of here. And Deon *will* die by my hands. Being alone for long periods of time with nothing but the same thoughts will have you planning things in exquisite details. Like Deon's death.

He's beaten me with his hands and feet. My body barely heals from the injuries before he's beating me again. Sometimes I pass out from the pain, but each time, I welcome the reprieve from this misery. It's amazing that I'm still sane, still breathing, still able to endure all of this.

He rips into me, and it takes everything for me not to pray for death. That would be better than having to continuously endure this violation. The theft of my body is worse than any blow from his fists.

Deon thinks just because I beg for food and water or show gratitude for the clothing he brings me, that my appreciation will somehow turn into love. I know he thinks by taking away the very things that make me human, I'll willingly give him my body in exchange for them. That I'll somehow fall in love with him. He's sick, and no matter how long he holds me prisoner here, I will always hate him. If he's banking on some Stockholm Syndrome shit happening with me, he'll be waiting until I take my final breath.

What he doesn't understand is I may depend on him for survival, and he may have his way with my body, but I will never, ever give him my heart.

That already belongs to another...

FBI SPECIAL AGENT TAYLOR

Knight King.

He is one smug son of a bitch if I ever met one. I guess having more money than you could ever spend will do that to you. We don't have access to Knight's bank records yet, but if I had to guess, I'd say he has to be making multi-millions by the week from this clinic alone. Not to mention the other legal and *illegal* business ventures the Kings are involved with.

I try not to grind my teeth as I watch the patriarch of the King family, Kurtis King, walk out of the room like he's God himself.

Kian does everything in his power to avoid eye contact with me. I can tell by his reaction to seeing me that he hasn't told anyone in his family about his arrest. This makes me lift an eyebrow. Curiosity has me wondering why he's keeping that momentous secret from his family, especially when they're bound to find out sooner than later.

I look over at Knight who's wearing a smirk on his face, trying to taunt me. "Tell me, Agent Taylor, what brings you all the way down here to see me?"

I wipe the grin off his face with one sentence. "I heard your girlfriend is missing." I know I shouldn't be making light of a young woman's abduction, but I just can't stand the look on Knight's face.

His grin falters. "Do you have an update on Solanie?"

I can tell by the tone of his voice that he knows that I don't. I can almost feel the contempt radiating off this man. Little does he realize the feeling is mutual.

"I'm afraid I don't. That's the reason I'm here, Mr. King. I thought I could ask you a few questions."

His eyes narrow. "Go ahead." He looks at the expensive watch on his wrist, insinuating that I'm already wasting his time.

I pull out a notepad and pretend that I'm reading questions off it. "What can you tell me about Solanie James?"

He sighs too loudly. "We were in those beginning stages of building somethin' great, but somebody took her. I don't know who or why. I can't tell you anything more than I already told all the other cops that have asked me the same damn questions."

I grit my teeth as the desire to slap the arrogance right off this man surges.

"Uh hu," I say. "Is there anyone *you* could be associated with that would want to harm Solanie?"

His eyes bulge at my audacity. It's now that he realizes I'm not here about Solanie. No, this visit is *all* about him.

"Why, Agent Taylor, I have no idea what you mean by that. I'm just a regular ol' businessman. I don't have any enemies."

I make a show of looking around his elaborate office. "Mr. King, I wouldn't classify anything about you as regular."

He stares at me. "Why are you really here, sista?" He puts emphasis on the word "sista" as if I'm betraying my race by being a federal agent and questioning him.

"Look, I really am concerned about Solanie," I say genuinely. "The department is afraid that she may be the latest victim of The Beauty Butchers."

Finally, the smugness completely evaporates from Knight's face. For the first time since I walked in here, he's taking me seriously.

I play on his sudden change of demeanor. "If you care about Solanie like I think you do, you should work with us, Knight, and not against us."

The self-righteous look reappears on his face so quickly, it's like it never left. "I just told you that I don't know anything. I was hoping you were coming in here to tell me about some new developments in the case. But I see that you don't know shit."

I swallow hard, but I don't say anything.

"Solanie has a lot of people that love her and wanna see her back home safe, including me. So if I find out anything, your department will be my first area of contact," he finishes.

I've been doing this for a long time, so I can sniff out a lie hidden in a pile of words. And Knight King has just lied to me. What I can't figure out is why.

I sigh and stand up. I'm wasting time here. I have to meet with Chandie Tocks. This stop to see Knight has been absolutely worthless.

I look around his office, and this time I don't disguise the disgust in my voice. "You guys are pretty busy. You have a lot of people waiting just to get in the door."

"People are in pain," he says flatly. "We're a pain management clinic." He stands up. He really is a tall guy. If he wasn't knee deep in everything that goes against what I stand for, he would be attractive. Being this close to him, I can easily see why women are taken by this man.

"I hope you have some really good lawyers that have plausible explanations for the amount of prescriptions that are leaving this place by the hour."

Fuck it. I might as well lay all my cards on the table.

He chuckles. "Have a good day, Agent Taylor," he says, dismissing me from his presence.

There isn't much I can do without a warrant. I'm pissed, but I only have myself to blame. I don't know what I thought I'd accomplish by stopping by here. The only thing this little visit has done is make me hate Knight King even more.

"Make sure Kian doesn't forget his court date," I say as I head to the front door of Knight's office. I throw a look over my shoulder at Knight whose facial expression hasn't reacted to what I said. "Those gun charges hold a lengthy prison sentence, ya know?"

I don't bother waiting for a reaction. I walk away and hop into my car. I slam the door and try to settle the anger and nagging suspicion building inside of me. If my intuition is right, and it almost always is, I need to probe more into the missing case of Solanie James. I don't really believe she could be a victim of The Beauty Butchers. It's more likely that she found out the kind of man Knight really is and faked her disappearance to rid him from her life. Unfortunately, that's probably the only way a woman would be able to walk away from a man like Knight. Still, even after telling myself this, I can't shake the feelings of *what if*?

SOLANIE

I've been watching Deon, trying to learn his moods. He's unpredictable most of the time. One minute, he can be tolerable, the next he's insanely violent. My hate for him grows by the second. For stealing my life, stealing my body, and for being so meticulous in everything he does. Never once slipping up and presenting me the opportunity of escape.

Tonight, things have changed.

Tonight, he's finally made a mistake.

His first mistake was unlocking my ankle shackle. He's in a weirdly good mood. He's brought liquor down here. I've barely taken two sips, but he's had like four shots. He's off his game, and even though I know I'm in no way stronger than him, I may be able to cause him some damage.

He gets up to get a can of Coke to chase the brown liquor, his eyes dancing with excitement that I have to pretend to share. When he stands up to leave, he shocks me by looking over his shoulder and inviting me upstairs with him.

"You've been good lately," he says. "I want you to come upstairs and watch TV with me."

I don't have to fake excitement, because now it's dancing all in my veins. If he lets me out of this basement, it will be the biggest mistake he's ever made because I won't ever be back. Once I'm upstairs, I'm escaping from this house of horror.

I follow him upstairs and sit on the living room couch next to him. He flips through the channels while my eyes keep dotting to the front door, praying for the chance to be able to run out of it.

I'm sitting stiffly upright on the couch, pretending to watch the TV when my eyes are actually trying to locate an escape route, until I hear a familiar voice on the television. I almost get whiplash at how fast my neck turns to face the television screen.

"Shit," Deon mutters.

My eyes instantly well as I watch a candlelight vigil being held in my honor. A news reporter is interviewing my mother who is fighting to hold back sobs while Mariah and Candace stand on both sides of her.

"I won't give up," Momma says. "I will not give up until my baby is back home safe and sound."

Deon fiddles with the remote, and my eyes whiz through the crowd until they find the familiar face I was looking for. I can only savor the side profile of Knight, and even then, my vision is so blurry with tears that I can't fully appreciate his beauty.

Deon changes the channel, and it feels like my chest is about to collapse. I can't hold back my tears no matter how hard I try, and that's not very hard because I no longer give a fuck about whatever consequences Deon gives me tonight.

"Sorry about that," he says, and he has the nerve to be smiling. "I forgot they were doing that shit tonight… I didn't expect the news to be covering it…" His voice trails off.

The TV is now on some old western, and my brain feels like it's been turned to mush. I want to claw Deon's eyes out with my bare hands. Rage brands itself into me until my skin starts to burn. I don't think I've ever felt the emotion of hate so strongly before in my life. It's suffocating, demanding to be released in an outburst of violent rage.

I'm not sure how long I remain seated on the couch. Time seems to be on an endless loop. It isn't until I hear Deon snoring next to me that I'm able to snap out of my daze.

My heart jumps into the middle of my throat. Tears of excitement gather in the corners of my eyes, and I send a thanks up to heaven to God and my daddy because I know both of them must be looking out for me right now.

I don't have the luxury of time to think things through. Deon could wake up at any moment. I slowly lift off the couch and tiptoe toward the door, pushing past every fear that's trying to stop me. I have no idea what the passcode of the lock box on the door could be, but I know it's six digits because I've counted them every time Deon enters or leaves the basement.

My hands are shaky as I enter 123456. A red light blinks three times, announcing that's an incorrect passcode. Panic threatens to consume my soul with anxiety, but I push past my fear.

It's a long shot but this is Deon we're talking about, so I key in *my* birthdate, and my heart almost comes to a halt when it lights up green and I hear the door unlock. I look over my shoulder; Deon hasn't stirred. I swing the door open, and I don't even think. I just run!

I run with everything inside of me. I run for my life. My legs are tight with fear, but I keep running. It's dark outside, and I'm surrounded by woods, but I don't stop running. I don't know which direction leads to freedom, but I won't let that stop me.

My lungs burn, my feet throb, and my muscles are on the brink of exhaustion, but I keep running.

It feels like I've been running for miles on top of miles, but still, all I see is woods. I want to scream out of frustration, but I'm afraid Deon will somehow hear it.

My chest tightens, and my legs lock, giving out on me. I fall onto the ground, wheezing for air. No matter how hard I inhale, I can't seem to get enough air into my lungs.

Tears of frustration fall out of my eyes. I curse my body

for being so weak. I think of my daddy, and suddenly a jolt of adrenaline has me back on my feet. I sprint like a runner that's almost to the finish line.

But there's no finish line in front of me. I feel like I'm just running aimlessly, with freedom nowhere in sight.

Then I hear it.

The sound of dogs barking. My blood runs cold, and fear seizes all activity of my limbs.

It's Deon. He's somewhere behind me, and with the help of his dogs, he'll easily be able to find me.

So what's the point in still running?

The sound of the barking gets closer and closer. I keep running, though my brain is telling me it's in vain.

Then it happens, the dogs catch up to me. They surround me like I'm prey. I'd rather be taken out by them than return to the hell Deon has created for me.

The dog that had kept me company my first night here runs up to me and starts licking my feet. I cry out in defeat; he'll never know just how bad he's betrayed me.

I see the flashlight, and my body wants to bolt, but I'm too exhausted.

Weak and defeated.

"Solanie!" Deon's voice is sinister. He's shaking his head and shaking the flashlight, casting an ominous glow throughout the woods. "You thought you could run from me, bitch?"

He drags me back toward hell. I'm kicking and screaming, but Deon is unfazed. We arrive back at the house much quicker than it'd taken me to run, making me realize I hadn't gotten far at all.

He throws me down the stairs into the basement, and I fall onto the floor in a defeated heap. It's getting so hard not to just give the fuck up. It's getting so hard to keep fighting.

Deon returns to the basement with a broom in his hand and fire in his eyes.

"You fucked up when you did that shit." He stalks toward me, and I cower under his domineering glare.

"There's consequences to disobedience," he says. He's staring at the broom in his hands, and I don't want to even think about what he plans on doing with it, but deep down inside, I know.

My body tries to revolt when he grabs me by my bleeding feet, made bloody from my barefoot run. He pulls me toward him and forces my legs open.

My mind goes numb, and by the grace of God, I don't feel what happens next. I see what he's doing, and I hear his vile, disgusting words. I taste the salt of my tears, but I'm detached, I'm no longer even here. I'm back in my childhood home, sitting in the backyard, drinking strawberry lemonade with my daddy. He's wiping away all my tears and telling me everything is going to be alright.

KNIGHT

Kian and I are at the club a couple of hours before our employees start showing up. Kian is dressed in all black. He's in his element. He's been grinning non-stop, and it's giving me pause. I'm worried that my brother takes too much pleasure in shit that most people wouldn't have the stomach for.

"You alright, my nigga?" I ask him.

He's still grinning. "Hell yeah. I can't wait to make this nigga regret the day he fucked with a King."

I have to admit, there's nobody else I'd rather have by my side while doing some gangsta shit, on my mission for vengeance.

It took two long ass weeks for Rax to get me a specific address. He said the delay was because the nigga was using a camouflaged IP. But Rax is a real one and was able to weed through all the coding and get me the exact address. Turns out, the real address wasn't anywhere near Katy.

"I know exactly where this is at, too," Kian had said. Of course, he did. And for once, I wasn't bothered about my brother's love of the hood.

I pour us shots, but Kian refuses. "I don't like to drink before work. Need my head clear and my reflexes fast."

I take both shots. It's been so long since I've done anything like this. I'd always hoped I'd never be reduced back to shit like this, but I'll come out of retirement twenty times over to get Solanie back.

After Rax got inside Solanie's apartment, he reported back to us that he'd found ten hidden cameras, almost two in every room. I knew then my return from retirement would be a bloody one.

Now I have the address to where the nigga that was stalking her lays his head, the address to where he could be keeping her. I ignore the voice in the back of my head telling me she's probably already dead, because every time I listen to it, I feel an overwhelming sense of loss of what could have been.

"I don't think I've ever seen that look on your face before," Kian says, stealing me from my dark thoughts.

"I got a lot on my mind," I tell him.

He nods like he knows the half.

"Starting with wondering why a fed bitch came up in my office talkin' 'bout they got you on some gun charges."

Kian's mouth falls open about as wide as his eyes. "Huh?"

"Huh?" I run my hand over my head to keep from spazzing out on his lil' ass.

"Shit," he says as he drops his eyes. "My bad, bro. I was gonna tell you."

"Man, what the fuck, Kian! What the fuck was you thinking?"

He shrugs. "I wasn't. I fucked up."

"You can't afford to fuck up like this, Kian! This is the fuck up of the century!"

"Man, I know! It was all a set up. They was using me to get to you," he says. "Thought if they got me on some bullshit ass charges, I would give them something on you to get out of it."

I lift my eyebrow.

He smirks. "Guess they don't know Kings never fold."

"Why you just now telling me this, Kian?"

He shrugs again. "I'on know, Knight. Kaleb told me not to. He said he was working on getting the charges dropped, so it wasn't no point in tellin' you or Pops."

I shake my head and chuckle out of frustration. "You got Kaleb involved in this bullshit too?"

"Kaleb is the best lawyer in Houston. The fuck else I was gonna call?"

This merits a real chuckle out of me. He's right, and if Kaleb thinks he can get the charges dropped, then there really isn't anything to be worried about. A little of the stress in my back and shoulders leaves, but the bulk of it will remain until I have Solanie back in my arms.

"Let me handle this, Knight," he says, his voice pleading with me. "Please."

"I ain't getting involved with your bullshit, Kian. I got enough on my plate right now. Fuckin' feds breathing down my neck... this shit with Solanie..."

"We gonna get Solanie back," Kian says as if it's a fact.

Kurtis enters from the back door of the club with Kaleb and Ma. Kian and I quickly change the subject while I make a mental reminder to check Kaleb's ass later on for keeping all of this from me.

"I got y'all a car." Kaleb tosses a pair of keys to Kian.

"We'll be two cars behind you to make sure you don't have a tail," Momma says. "We'll fall back once you get on Forty-five. There are two lookouts at your destination right now, waiting on y'all."

"You can contact them by calling the only number in the contact list on this phone." Kurtis hands me a cheap flip phone.

"I would volunteer to come along but..." Kaleb says, and we all break out into laughter.

I'm grateful to Kaleb for lifting the mood. It's been so long since I had a real good laugh. It seems like shit has been falling apart all around me ever since Solanie disappeared. My thoughts have been torturous, wondering if she's still alive or... now that I know she had a stalker, I don't even want to imagine the things he's done to her.

"Knight? Did you hear me?" Momma says.

"Oh, my bad, Ma. What was you saying?"

I know she can tell I'm a million miles away. She grabs both sides of my face and kisses my forehead, something she hasn't done since I was a lil' kid. "Be careful. Please." With that, she exits.

I look over to see what Pops is talking about, but I can't hear what he's saying to Kian. When he's done talking, he turns to me, and the corners of his mouth rise into half of a grin. "You know, we have plenty of people who can handle this, Knight. You don't have to be the one to go over there."

I give him a look, but I don't say anything because if I do, it will definitely be disrespectful.

Kurtis reads my facial expression and laughs. "Yeah, yeah, I already know. 'Cause once upon a time, I was in love too."

We all laugh at him.

"Let me finish," he says, but his voice is playful. "I once was in love with ya Momma, and it wasn't nothing nobody could tell me." His voice goes solemn. "It was also nothing I wouldn't do *for* her. So trust me, son. If don't nobody know what it means for you to do what you about to do, I know. Shit, I wanna hop in the back seat and join y'all." He laughs before falling quiet, and his eyes are thoughtful.

He looks at me, and his silence says a lot more than the speech he'd just given.

The sound of loud banging at the front entrance of the club draws all of our attention.

"What the fuck?" Kian pulls out a gun.

I squint my eyes, trying to make out who's at the front door beating on the door trying to get in.

"Do you know them?" Kaleb asks.

I walk toward the door, and I instantly recognize the two women at the door as Solanie's best friends.

"Let us in!" Candace hollers. "We need to talk to you, Knight!"

"Shit," I say under my breath. I can't stomach having to look them in their faces knowing I still haven't brought Solanie home. I don't need the pain in their eyes to remind me that I'm failing them.

I unlock the door of the club and let them come inside.

"We've been trying to get in touch with you for like forever now!" Mariah says.

"Uh..." I don't even know what to say to them.

"We're out, Knight. Keep us updated," Kurtis turns to leave, and Kaleb hesitates before following him out the back door.

Kian walks up to my side. "What's up?"

Candace and Mariah's faces go flush at Kian's appearance. I know shit just got a lot more awkward seeing as though he never called Mariah after getting her number. I can tell by the sudden shift in her body language that she feels some type of way about that. But she just doesn't know the shitstorm she avoided by not getting close to my brother.

"We wanted to thank you for the reward you put out," Candace says.

"Yeah," Mariah says. "We appreciate you doing that." Her eyes quickly look at Kian before diverting just as fast. "And Solanie's momma really did too."

"It ain't nothing. It's the least I could do." I think back to how uncomfortable it was meeting Solanie's momma and step-daddy at the vigil. I hated with everything in me that I was meeting them under those circumstances.

Mariah burst into tears, and I ain't talking one of those pretty cries, either. Her whole body starts shaking. Candace tried to comfort her, but Kian pulls her into his arms.

"Sssssh, it's alright," he tries to soothe her. "We gonna find out what the fuck happened."

"That's my best friend," she cries. "I'm talking since elementary school. She's like a sister to me. I don't know what I would do without her."

That's all it takes for Candace to start crying too. This is the last thing I need right now. I place my arm over her shoulder, feeling awkward as shit at my weak attempt at comfort.

"We love that damn girl to death," Candace says. "I just can't understand why this happened to her. I done asked myself a thousand times who in the hell would want to do something to her, but I still can't find the answer."

I've also asked myself that a million times. But now, I have the address of the fucker burning a hole in my pocket.

Grief pours out of Solanie's two best friends as they profess their love for her. I feel robbed of the chance to get to really know her. I'm not a fool; I know if a person isn't found within seventy-two hours, they're more than likely dead. That thought feels like someone just pulled the trigger on a gun aimed straight at my heart.

I didn't get the chance to show Solanie how different I am from the last fuck nigga that broke her heart. I didn't protect her...

I know I'm rude as hell by how I abruptly pull away from Candace, but time is ticking, and I got a nigga I need to skin alive. "Look, we were just on our way out..."

Candace sniffles and runs the sleeve of her jacket across her nose. She nods her head like she understands, but I know she doesn't. I'm being rude by rushing them off, but I need to get out of here. Their tears and grief are making me acknowledge my own, after weeks of suppressing my emotions.

Kian whispers something that has Mariah laughing through her tears. I have to give it to my brother; he's handling this comfort thing a lot better than I am.

"Okay, we'll let you go. But please, if you hear anything, let the police handle it," Mariah says.

I nod at her, and Mariah's eyes search mine for deception, so I look away. I've always been bad at lying, and I'm afraid she'll be able to see what I'm on my way to do.

I'm relieved when they finally leave.

Kian watches them until their car disappears down the street. He turns and looks at me. "You ready to do this shit, big bro?"

I throw the duffle bag over my shoulder and give him a look. "Been ready."

We exit out the back and see a green Ford Focus parked outside. Kian hits the unlock on the keychain and scowls. "Fuckin' Kaleb plays too much!"

I burst into laughter, and it feels good in contrast to the rage that's made my body it's permanent home.

"We gonna look like clowns getting out of this small ass car!" Kian huffs as he opens the driver's door. "I can't even fit in this shit!"

Both of us struggle to get inside of the car while adjusting the seats as far back as possible and cussing out our little brother for his lil' idea of being funny.

I scan the scene, peeping our lookouts in two black Lincolns across the street.

I get a rush thinking I could possibly be this close to Solanie. Kian and I don't say anything as we get out of the car and head straight for apartment 902. Niggas notice us but turn their heads, knowing better than to be caught staring.

I can't wait to get this shit over with.

It feels like hours before we finally find the apartment. I look around as Kian plays with the locks. It easily gives in to whatever he's doing, and we slip inside the apartment without being noticed by any nosy bystanders.

As soon as we enter the apartment, I can tell the nigga that lives here hasn't been here in a while. My shoulders slump in disappointment of not coming face to face with the motherfucker that's been stalking my girl. Whether he was involved with her disappearance or not, the nigga was gonna die tonight.

"This nigga nasty as hell," Kian says as he walks through the small living room. There are half eaten bowls of cereal sitting on the coffee table, the souring milk reeking the whole place up. There's a worn-out couch that he probably got from sitting outside some trash dumpster. I wouldn't sit on the shit if somebody paid me.

Kian picks up an envelope from a pile of unopened mail. "Deon."

I squint my eyes at the revelation. I finally have a name to put to the faceless man that haunts my dreams. Every night, I dream of him screaming out for mercy that I'll refuse to give.

Kian tosses the envelope at me, and I catch it and place it in the inside pocket of my jacket. By this time tomorrow, I'll know everything there is to know about this Deon cat.

I walk into the bedroom of the apartment that's even smaller than the living room. My eyes scan the room for any clues that will lead to Solanie's whereabouts. I freeze in place when I come across what looks like a shrine to Solanie.

"What the fuck?" I hear Kian behind me, his eyes on the same thing that has my attention.

There are twelve photos of Solanie pinned to the wall in the corner of the room. Under the photos is a small, cluttered desk. I recognize one of the items as the brand of perfume that Solanie wears. There's a sock, a pair of lace underwear, two necklaces, a fucking used tampon, a hairbrush, and an empty bottle of Victoria Secret lotion. I know all of these things belong to Solanie, and now I also know the kind of fucked-up person we're dealing with.

"This nigga is crazy as hell, bro." Kian's face is curled in disgust.

"And he has Solanie." If I doubted it before, looking at this shrine erases all doubt.

"Damn." Kian sighs. "You wanna wait here for his ass?"

"Naw." I shake my head. "I got other plans."

I look around the room one more time before making my exit. As soon as I'm outside, I hit Rax up. "I got a name. I need you to find everything you can on this muthafucka."

I walk back to our clown car, but before I can hop in somebody is calling my name. Me and Kian look over our shoulder to see some lil' dude running up to us.

"Say, what it do, Knight?" The smile on his face is goofy and irritating my already agitated mood. He looks over at Kian and says, "Kian, my nigga. What's good?"

"Say, this ain't a good time right now," Kian warns him.

"Aw, man! I got two Kings in my neighborhood. I just wanna say wassup! I mean, it ain't everyday you see a King in Sunnyside!"

"Man, it ain't a good time, bro," Kian repeats.

The nigga must be hard of hearing because he runs up closer to us on some groupie shit with his hands extended, and all I see is red.

The first blow I throw knocks him right off his feet. The second one knocks a couple of his teeth out. As I pummel this fool, the only thing I see is that sick ass shrine to Solanie, and for now, this nigga is Deon.

I'm not sure how many times I hit this guy before Kian finally pulls me off him. "Chill out, Knight! Chill out!"

My rage is settled, and beating the shit out of this nigga won't bring Solanie back to me any faster. I leave him bleeding in the middle of the street and head back to the car. I look over at Kian and say, "Send somebody to clean up everything back there in that shithole. I don't want any link to Solanie left in that nigga's apartment."

Kian nods his understanding.

The last thing I need is for the cops to find anything in Deon's apartment related to his obsession with Solanie. They'll just fuck everything up, and I need to get my hands on him first.

Kian jogs across the street to let our lookouts know to stay the night and hit us up immediately if anyone enters apartment 902.

DEON

Solanie still doesn't know how to behave. She doesn't realize just how easy it would be for me to just kill her. I've never kept a woman for more than four days. Solanie has made it weeks beyond her expiration date.

I've been waiting for Nate to show up. It's been two weeks since he popped up over here, and I haven't talked to him since. Not for his lack of trying to reach out to me; I just don't answer his calls.

Because of Solanie's escape attempt, I've had to stop going into town as much. I've had to beat her back in submission. I've had to do things in hopes of breaking her spirit. But that glimmer of hope is always still fucking there in her eyes. I think it has something to do with that news coverage of that candlelight vigil her mother and stepdaddy held for her. She broke down seeing all the people she loves on TV, crying and pleading for her safe return. Even that nigga Knight was there. When the camera panned across the crowd, I was shocked to see how many people love her.

But now, weeks later, the news hardly ever mentions her. The world has moved on and has almost completely forgotten her. I don't know how that is possible when there is absolutely nothing forgettable about Solanie, but the media doesn't mention her anymore.

I told her the police only have so many resources that they can devote to finding a missing person, especially when so many other crimes are happening every day. Not to mention,

The Beauty Butcher's latest victim.

Nate's, not mine.

I haven't went hunting since I took Solanie. What's the point? She's all I need, and the desire to hurt anybody else has vanished. I wish Nate could find the same satisfaction in a woman in the same way that I've found it in Solanie. Maybe then he would understand why I want to keep her. Maybe then he would stop blowing up my fucking phone.

It's been a couple of hours since I've been downstairs to check up on Solanie, so I head down there now. As soon as I enter the basement, she stands up. It's something I've trained her to do.

Good girl.

Her eyes are jumpy and nervous. I don't even make it halfway to her before I hear loud banging on the front door. Even though I'm surprised by the knocking, I don't trip because I know who it is. I grit my teeth and tell Solanie not to go anywhere, as if she could.

I head back upstairs and open the door for Nate. He rushes past me in a ball of fury. He looks around before turning his wrath on me. "Why haven't you been answering my got-damn calls?"

I don't owe him an explanation. I'm a grown ass man. "I've been busy."

I can't remember the last time I've seen Nate this pissed off. His nostrils are flared, and his eyes are bulging. He points toward the basement. "Did you know that bitch belongs to Knight King?"

I decide to forgive him for saying Solanie belongs to anyone other than me. "Who the hell is Knight King?" I pretend the name is foreign to me, and the nigga's name taste like shit coming off my tongue.

Nate runs his hands over his head. I recognize this as an exercise he does to settle his temper. "Someone we really don't want to fuck with, Deon. I hope you didn't willingly take a bitch from a man like that."

I shrug and hope my face is convincing. "I don't even know who you talking about."

Nate runs his hand across his balding head again. "Knight has a reward out for any information about her disappearance. It's been all over the news! Why don't you ever watch the fucking news?"

I have been watching the news. I just don't sit in front of a television for hours on end like Nate does. This is the first time I've heard of some reward being out for Solanie. That fucking Knight! I should have killed him when I had the chance.

"Nate, I swear I didn't know nothing about no reward or the guy that's offering it."

He shakes his head like he doesn't know if he should believe me or not. "Dammit, Deon." He sits on the edge of the couch and buries his face into his hands. "You have no idea the shit you put us in by taking this girl. I hope you not lying straight to my face when you say you didn't know who she belonged to."

I grit my teeth and literally bite my tongue to keep from correcting my brother. She doesn't fucking belong to anyone but me. *She's mine.*

Nate sighs. "Then again, I know you ain't dumb enough to pursue her knowing she was in any way involved with somebody like Knight King."

"Who the fuck is Knight?" I say through clenched teeth.

Nate shakes his head like I'm a dumb ass and doesn't bother answering me. "I just hope you covered your tracks well enough that the nigga doesn't come looking for you."

"Haven't I always?"

Nate laughs. "You don't really want the answer to that." He sighs before saying, "I hope she's worth all of this fucking trouble."

"She is," I retort before I can stop myself. I realize it was a mistake by the scowl that's now on Nate's face.

"When are you going to get rid of her?" His voice is low and his face emotionless. "You done had her too long. She should've already been dead."

"I ain't ready to kill her yet," I tell him.

Nate jumps up from the couch and is in my face in a matter of seconds. "What's wrong with you? What you mean you ain't ready to kill her yet? I can smell the fucking weakness on you. That bitch is making you weak. I don't even think you have it in you to kill her, do you?" He doesn't give me the chance to answer him before he's talking again. "Shit! I'm going to have to do it, ain't I? I'm gonna have to slice this bitch up by my damn self, huh?"

I can feel myself going into fight or flight mode. Nate is tossing out too many threats, and I know my brother well enough to know they aren't empty.

"I don't need your help," I spit. "Have I ever needed your help?"

Nate laughs. "Oh, you don't want to go there do you, lil' brother?"

"You ain't perfect ya self, Nate!" I feel the need to remind him. "Your latest screw up is all over the news too. What happened to you taking a hiatus? You couldn't even hold out two weeks. The media is calling your latest kill the most gruesome assault The Beauty Butchers have ever committed."

Now, Nate doesn't have so much to say. He walks toward the door to leave after being put in his place. He grabs the door handle but stops and turns to glower at me. His voice is unusually calm when he finally speaks. "I love you brother, I really do. But if she's still breathing the next time I come over here, I'm going to make sure she isn't by the time that I leave."

I slam the door behind him. I spit out a hundred cuss words and look toward the basement door. I can't believe what I have to do.

Solanie has to die.

FBI SPECIAL AGENT TAYLOR

After my disastrous visit to Knight King's clinic, I hopped on the freeway to interview Chandie Tocks, only for her to call me and cancel at the last minute. We've been playing phone tag for the last couple of weeks, but finally, I'm able to sit down with the woman. After the Beauty Butchers' last victim, I need this to not be a dead end. I need whatever Chandie has to say to lead me straight to those motherfuckers' doors. Because they're getting more brutal, more violent, more ruthless.

Chandie invites me inside her stale-smelling home and sits across from me, crossing her varicose vein riddled legs. She lights a cigarette and asks, "So, y'all gonna reopen Rochelle's case?"

I pull out my notes. "I've taken a look at it, Miss Tocks."

"Call me Chandie. Miss Tocks sounds like you talkin' to my momma or some shit."

"Okay, Chandie," I say. "Tell me more about Rochelle. You were close friends, correct?"

"That's right. We both ran away from home. Got tired of listening to our parents, tired of the rules, curfews, and all that stuff that at the time was good for us, but we didn't know." She pauses to take a long drag from her cigarette.

She continues, "We just thought we was grown. Thought it would be easy to get an apartment and live by our own rules, ya know. It was harder than we thought, and soon we ran outta money and options. We was young and dumb and didn't know no better. We hooked up with chick named Corin and shoulda ran the other way 'cause she got us into prostitution. Worst decision we ever made." Chandie's voice cracks, and she stops to collect herself.

"That's why I went down to the police station. See, back then, Rochelle and me was hooking, and there was this man that used to come by the stroll like every other day. Mufucka was creepy looking, but Corin said he was a regular and he was harmless. Harmless my ass! First time I saw him, I knew something wasn't right with him. But what made me really sure something was wrong with his ass was when he started popping up with two lil' boys in the back seat of his car, talkin' 'bout they was his sons. Lil' boys couldn't have been no more than eleven or twelve. Who does that kinda shit?"

"This all sounds terrible, Chandie. But I have to ask, what does this have to do with The Beauty Butcher?"

She eyeballs me. "I'm gettin' to that part." She takes another long pull from her cigarette, and then she says, "I started gettin' scared when girls started disappearing and never coming back. Then, we started hearing stories about them being found dead with their faces all cut up. I started carrying a weapon on me 'cause I wasn't tryin' to be next. When that weirdo came by the stroll, I begged Rochelle not to get in the car with him, but she did it anyway. Never saw her again. I told the cops all of this way back then. I told them about that crazy looking mufucka and how I just knew he was the one who killed Rochelle. But they didn't do nothing about it. Whole thing scared me so bad, I went back home to my parents."

I'm sure I didn't read any of what Chandie has just told me in Rochelle's case files. My hand feels like it's about to cramp up by how fast I'm taking notes. Multiple women killed with their faces cut up? A bone chilling sensation runs down my spine.

"This man you say you believe was responsible, can you describe him?"

Chandie closes her eyes. "He was a lil' taller than me. Light skinned, ugly as hell, with a pot belly. He was probably forty-something, and he had some purple ass gums you couldn't help but stare at every time he opened his mouth."

"If I showed you some photographs, do you think you'd be able to pick him out?"

"Hell yeah!" Chandie puts her cigarette out in an already full ashtray. "A guy that creepy looking, I'll never forget."

I thank Chandie for her time and get up to leave her home. She walks me to the door and before I can leave, she stops me by placing her hand on my arm.

"Rochelle wasn't perfect, but she didn't deserve to die for her mistakes. She was young, and I'm sure in time she woulda pulled her head back on straight. I hope you reopen her case and find who killed her. It's been eighteen years, and her parents died never knowing who killed their baby."

I give Chandie my word that I'll look into everything she's told me and walk back to my car. My mind is reeling. I flip through pages of Rochelle's case files, not being able to find anything about similar murders of prostitutes happening around the same time Rochelle was killed.

We could have had a serial killer eighteen plus years ago that was targeting prostitutes. Their line of work possibly made it harder for police to connect the similarities.

Some of the things Chandie said keep echoing loudly in my ears. The guy came to pick up and kill hookers with his two young sons in the back seat? Multiple women found with their faces mutilated?

The wheels in my brain are turning so fast that I feel dizzy. The man Chandie described would be too old now to still be committing those crimes. But not his sons... The timeline adds up, making them around the same age the FBI profiler had estimated. The brutality is too similar to ignore. Could it be possible those two little boys grew up to be The Beauty Butchers?

My cop's intuition is telling me that solving this cold case will not only bring closure to Rochelle's case and solve a boatload of other similar cold cases, but it'll also lead me straight to The Beauty Butchers.

SOLANIE

Every part of my body hurts. The physical pain pales in comparison to the emotional wreckage of my mind and heart. I've been trapped here for so long I've lost any sense of time. Weeks, months, or years could have gone by for all I know. Day in and day out, I'm forced to endure unimaginable things.

Every day, I fight against my own mind when it tells me to give up. When it tells me I can't go on anymore, I push through by holding on with an ironclad grip to a fading hope of rescue.

Deon has convinced himself that I love him. I have to placate him because he's gentler when he believes my faux affection is real. Sometimes, he comes at me angry for no reason and takes that anger out on me in horrifying ways. He gets off on my fear, my pain, and my overpowering despair.

Sleep evades me, no matter how much I beg for it. It's my only escape from this hell. It's also the only way that I can see Knight. It's been so long since I've seen him that his facial features are starting to blur in my head. I fear the day that I completely forget the way he looks. One thing that will forever be etched in my heart though, is the way that he made me feel. That's something Deon will never be able to take from me, no matter how hard he tries.

Back when I was free, I remember seeing on the news how he butchered his victims without mercy. I'm not sure why he hasn't killed me by now. He rants on and on about how his brother won't allow him to keep me. I can sense I'm closer to death than I've ever been. The fear that used to accompany that thought has long left me. Now, all I feel is peace because I just want this to be over.

If death is my only way to be free of Deon, I'll gladly take it. Even though it hurts so bad to think about never seeing my parents again or laughing with my girls.

Not seeing Knight just one more time...

Deon robbed me of a future. Even if I do make it out of here, what kind of woman will I be? Dark memories of my time spent here would haunt me, leaving me a shell of the person that I used to be. Maybe death is the best option.

Tears fall down my face at this realization. My hate for Deon grows, even though I'm not sure how it's possible to hate him any more than I already do.

My pulse quickens as I hear him enter the basement. I know I'm supposed to stand to greet him, but I'm tired.

So tired.

Tired of placating him in hopes that he won't hurt me. Tired of camouflaging the hate in my eyes when he looks at me. Tired of forcing my mind to go to other places when he robs my body of what it would never willingly give to him.

I could fight. I could try to take him for once and for all, but he feeds me the bare minimum ensuring I'll never have enough strength to throw a blow with any real power.

"Solanie." His voice is agitated because I've disobeyed him by not greeting him.

I keep my back to him, ignoring him because I know why he's here. My body is crying for a reprieve. I'm not sure I can bear him touching me right now.

"Solanie!" he screams at me.

I jump at the force behind his voice, and even though I don't want to, I turn around and look at him. This time, hoping he not only sees my hate but feels it too.

He's shaking his head at me. It's easy to see today is one of his angry days. Desolation hits the bottom of my heart.

"Nate says I can't keep you anymore."

I stare blankly back at him with unblinking eyes.

"I want to keep you, Solanie. Please believe me when I say there's nothing more in the world that I want more. But rules are rules, and we haven't gotten this far without following them."

He starts walking toward me. The closer he gets, the more it feels like a thousand spiders are crawling down my back.

"Just get it over with," I tell him. He wants my fear, but I refuse to give it to him any longer.

"You were the best, you know? I would have kept you forever if it was up to me. But Nate is right. The longer I keep you around, the risker it becomes. The cops are working on leads and shit right now." He shakes his head. "I fucked up, so losing you is the punishment for my mistakes."

It's then that I see the long blade in his hands.

So this is it? This is how I'll meet death. I was hoping it'd be something quick. Something I wouldn't have to feel. I've felt too much pain these last few weeks. Agony rips through my body, reminding me of all the ways that Deon has hurt me.

"Trust me, I don't want to do this," he says, but the smile on his face conflicts with his words.

He kneels down, and I consider trying to yank the knife out of his hands. Hell, I might as well go down fighting!

I instantly reach out and try to grab it, but he reacts just as fast and tries to evade my hands. My hand grabs onto the blade and I pull as hard as I can, ignoring the sensation of the blade slicing into my palm. An animalistic growl escapes my mouth as I pull strength from somewhere deep inside of me. I can feel Deon losing his grip on the knife, and adrenaline gives me the extra power I need to keep tugging.

But it's useless.

Deon is stronger than me, and he effortlessly snatches the knife out of my grip. I instantly feel the knife slashing into my hand. I don't have time to concentrate on that throbbing pain because within seconds Deon plunges the knife into my stomach.

I yelp in surprise, shock, and terror. I stare at the thing sticking out of my abdomen, and everything about this feels unreal. I look up at Deon and he's looking like he's in a trance.

"Help me." I try to reach some kind of humanity inside of him.

My pleas are futile because Deon has already proven he has no humanity. He turns around and walks out of the basement, leaving me to die.

KNIGHT

As soon as my cell rings, I almost knock everything off my nightstand to grab it.

"Yeah?" My voice is hoarse with sleep, but the eagerness in it is loud and clear.

"I just sent you everything," Rax says. His accent seems to be stronger over the phone. "Come to find out this bitch ass nigga is an interesting character. His family owns land out in Strope, about two hours from here. But you won't believe what else I found out about this cat, Knight..."

I'm half listening to Rax while fumbling with my laptop to open the email he just sent me. The computer seems to be fucking with me by moving extra slow.

"Can you believe that shit, my brother?" Rax says, his voice animated.

"Hell naw. Shit's crazy," I say, even though I didn't hear a thing he just said.

"Take care of your business, young King," he says before disconnecting the call.

When the email finally loads, I have everything I need to know about this Deon dude, including his latest DMV photo. I almost start coughing in surprise when I immediately recognize this motherfucker! The weirdo looking ass nigga staring at me from my computer screen is the same fucking nigga that smashed into the back of my car and gave me some bogus ass insurance information. I'd been pissed completely off but didn't have the time to go hunting his ass down. I just paid to get my shit fixed and hadn't thought twice about it since.

Now I'm punched with the realization that this is the same nigga that was stalking Solanie and snatched her from my front door.

I go on autopilot, calling Kurtis and then Kian. Kurtis doesn't give me the option of handling this shit on my own. He's already solicited the help of a few niggas that owe him more than a few favors.

Wrath drives my movements as I get dressed and pack my duffle bag full of the items that I'll need. I take another look at the address of the land that Rax said this nigga owned. It's quite a distance from here but I wouldn't care if it was states away. I have a feeling this is exactly where I'll find Solanie—dead or alive.

Kian is at my door by the time I'm prepared to leave. I don't recognize the niggas in the two Suburban SUVs parked out front, but I appreciate their willingness to drop everything to help me out. I don't know what I'm about to walk into, but I'll willingly walk into a burning house to get Solanie.

Kian doesn't say anything, he just reaches for my duffle and heads toward one of the Suburbans.

I take a deep breath. "I'm coming, Solanie," I say before following Kian to the truck. "I'm coming to get you, baby."

By the time we arrive, it feels like we've been driving for days. I'm restless, anxious, and high off adrenaline. The last time was a dummy mission, but I'm not leaving this house until I have Deon's blood on my hands.

"You think he in that piece of shit house down there?" Kian points down the street.

We're parked some distance away from a small shack. It's the only house we've been able to see for miles. I'm not even sure if we're in the right area. Our GPS stopped working a good while ago, and we're in the middle of the boonies.

"I don't know," I answer him. "But we're about to find out."

I look over my shoulder at my father's henchmen. They are all armed with weapons that should be outlawed and waiting on me to give a command.

"We gonna go 'round the back," I tell them. "Two of y'all hang out here, and watch for anything that looks out of pocket. Y'all other two, head toward the front."

The Suburban behind us pulls up to our window, the driver rolls down his window. "The house up there is on fire."

"Fire!" Kian and I say at the same time.

Without hesitation, Kian smashes on the gas. We pull up right in front of the shack, and I hop out before we even come to a full stop. All of the earlier instructions I'd just given are completely forgotten as Kian and I race toward the house.

I can see smoke billowing over the house, but I can't see the flames. I exchange glances with Kian before kicking the front door in. It doesn't budge, so Kian and I kick it at the same time, and it gives in to our strength.

I cover my mouth and nose with my shirt as soon as the smoke hits me. I see flames that are quickly gaining force. Fear momentarily paralyzes me before the thought of Solanie burning to death causes me to run headfirst into a death trap.

"Solanie!" I'm not sure if she can hear me, if she's even here, but I won't let this house burn down until I'm sure she isn't in it.

"Solanie!" I hear Kian calling out behind me.

I want to tell him to go back to the truck, to let me handle this on my own, but I already know there's no way he's leaving my side.

We move as quickly as we can throughout the house that's on the verge of collapsing. I pray we're not about to collapse with it due to smoke inhalation. I spot some steps in the back of the house and head toward them while trying not to inhale too deeply.

"Yo, Knight! We need to get out of here!" Kian calls after me.

I know he's right, but I can't turn around now. I look at him and notice two of the men we came with are standing behind him, coughing and turning back. I don't have the luxury of time to debate my next move.

I ignore Kian and walk down the small steps and kick the door with all my strength. It breaks open upon impact and what I see in that room makes my heart split in two separate pieces.

Solanie.

She's lying on the floor unmoving. I rush to her and when I turn her over, I see a gigantic knife sticking out of her stomach.

"Fuck!"

I pick her up and cradle her while trying not to touch the knife. I don't know if she's still alive, but I'd fucking die before I leave her here to burn in this house.

"Solanie, baby, I'm here," I tell her, praying my voice can somehow reach her.

I race back up those stairs like a gold medalist track star. The fire has gotten worse, and it's looking impossible that we'll make it out the same door that I entered. I frantically look around, but there aren't any windows we could escape out of.

"Fuck!" I bellow out in frustration. I'm feeling weaker by the second, and Solanie is starting to feel like dead weight in my arms. I know I need to get the fuck out of here quick.

Everything about my body feels heavy, but I didn't come this far to let a fire take me down. I see a door in my peripheral, but I can also see flames all around it.

Fuck it.

I run toward that door at full speed and aim my shoulder at it. I don't know if I've suddenly been blessed with supernatural strength, or if the fire had made the door weaker, because it gives easily.

I tumble out of the house and am greeted by the sounds of dogs barking. I get as far from the house as I can before I collapse onto the ground.

"Knight?"

The sound of her voice gives me a second wind. She's fighting to keep her eyes open. "Don't talk," I tell her. I look up and see Kian driving toward us at a high speed.

"Knight?" she says again. "Am I dreaming? Are you really here?"

"Yeah. I'm here, baby." I wipe away the hair that's stuck to her wet forehead. She starts coughing up blood, and the realization that I could lose her feels worse than the thought of finding her dead. "Stay with me, Solanie. Please, baby. I need you to stay with me."

I can tell she's in pain by the way her facial expression squeezes together. Then her lips turn up into the faintest of smiles and she says, "You really are a knight… My Knight."

Kian and three of the guys are jumping out of the truck. They're taking her from my arms. I feel like I'm outside of my body watching all of this happen, and I don't even know how I got back inside the Suburban.

"Hold on, Solanie!" Kian hollers as he puts the truck in reverse. He looks over at me before he rams on the gas, sending the truck in reverse at a high speed. "She gon' make it, bro. She gon' make it."

I close my eyes and pray that his words can reach all the way up to God's ears.

FBI SPECIAL AGENT TAYLOR

I'm knee deep in cold cases. I've put together at least fifteen who were prostitutes, killed, and left with their faces mutilated. There's so many of them that it's hard to believe they weren't linked together before now. I feel sick to my stomach thinking whoever was behind all these crimes could have bred two more serial killers, mimicking their father. The only striking difference is our victims today aren't prostitutes. That doesn't deter me; I'm positive I'm onto something.

"Taylor, whatcha up to?" Mitchell stops by my desk.

I don't know why, but I quickly exit out of the page on my computer. I haven't told anyone about what I'm working on. If I'm right, this could be the case of the century. And I don't want Mitchell trying to ride my coattail or take any of the credit for my work. As bad as he's vying for a promotion, I'll be damned if he gets it off my hard work.

"Oh, nothing," I answer him. "Any luck on the store video tapes?"

He frowns. "Not at all. We've literally sat through so much footage that I never want to see the inside of another shoe store again."

I laugh at him, kind of grateful I hadn't been added to the task force searching through them.

"Well, I'm taking off early. Jess has a doctor appointment.

We're going to get one of those 3D ultrasound thingies. Have you heard of those? We're supposed to be able to see all the baby's facial features and stuff." Mitchell's eyes light up every time he talks about the child he and Jess tried so hard to conceive for so many years. They'd almost given up, almost stopped getting the expensive fertility treatments when their miracle finally happened.

"See ya Monday!" I call after him and he throws me the deuce over his shoulder.

Once he's gone, I return my attention to my computer, only to be disturbed again, but this time by Special Agent in Charge Johnson. His face is red, and his eyes have doubled in size. "Where's Mitchell?"

"Uh, he just left," I say. "What's up?"

"I think we got something on the tapes!" Johnson looks like he's about to explode with excitement.

"The Beauty Butcher? Oh my God!" I jump up from my chair so fast that it topples over. I follow Johnson into the conference room where most of the task unit is already seated. He tries calling Mitchell, but his call goes straight to voicemail.

"He's at the doctor's office with Jess," I tell them. "He probably turned his cell off." I kind of feel bad that Mitchell is missing this. He's been such a kiss ass lately, and it's just his luck that as soon as he leaves, he misses the perfect opportunity to stick his head up the boss's ass.

We watch the video in silence at least six times in a row. Our suspect is a black man with a medium build who is purchasing the shoes in the right size. His baseball cap is pulled so low over his face that we'll never be able to make a positive ID, but still this could be something great.

You think that's him?" somebody in the room asks

"Could be. He is purchasing the shoes in the exact size in question. I've sat through forty-six hours of video, and this is not only the first person to buy a pair of Ryde sneakers in a size ten, but he fits the profile."

"He paid in cash," I point out. I'm disappointed he wasn't dumb enough to buy the shoes with a credit card and lead us straight to him.

"Taylor, you think you can get this to the media?" Johnson asks me. "I want this fucker's face on every news channel by suppertime tonight."

I nod, and I'm already going through my cell phone for my media contacts. I'm interrupted when my phone starts ringing. I excuse myself and step out of the conference room when I see it's Detective Hardee.

"Hardee, tell me you're calling me with good news."

"Uh, possibly," he says. "You remember Knight King's girlfriend that went missing last month? Solanie James?"

"Of course."

"Well, she's been found."

"No shit?"

"Yeah. She's at a hospital in Strobe right now. I'm on my way over there right now. You want to tag along?"

Of course I fucking do! I'm just about to repeat those exact words to him when I remember I have to get the tapes to the local news stations.

"Uh, I'm kinda in the middle of something, Hardee. But please, call me when you're done, and let me know everything. Even if you think it's insignificant."

Detective Hardee sounds surprised by me turning this opportunity down. "Yeah, okay. Sure. You got it."

I hang up with him and head back into the conference room. I've got a long night ahead of me. For once, Knight King *has* to take the backburner.

DEON

She's perfect.

She doesn't look like Solanie, but she's still beautiful. Now that Solanie is dead, my monster has returned with a vengeance, hungry for fear and blood. Ready to wreak havoc because it no longer has Solanie.

My eyes follow this new chick as she leaves the gym and gets inside her car. I start my car up and follow her as she drives straight into a fast-food drive-thru line.

"Tsk tsk. That workout is going to be wasted on that greasy shit," I say, as if she can hear me. I laugh to myself and then my thoughts travel to how eager Solanie used to look when I brought her fast food. Remembering the things I could make her do for a greasy burger makes my dick jump.

I can't wait to take this next victim. She's no Solanie, but she'll do.

I hate to pull my eyes off her, but I have to when my cell starts ringing. I know it's Nate. He's the only person that ever calls me.

"Yes?" I'm annoyed he's calling and interrupting me. I hang back as she pays for her shitty food. As soon as she drives off, I'm close behind.

"Is it done?" he asks.

I don't hide the animosity in my voice when I answer him. "If you're asking if I killed her, yes I did, even though I didn't fuckin' want to."

"There's a lot of things I don't want to do, brother, but still, I have to do them on a daily basis. It's time you grew the fuck up."

"Fuck you!" I spit. I'm pissed he made me get rid of Solanie. She was the closest to perfection that I've ever been, and now I have to settle for a chick who eats fast food minutes after leaving the gym.

"How did you do it?"

I don't tell him the truth. He expects me to have carved Solanie up like we do all of our victims, but Solanie was different. She didn't deserve to be treated like all the others. So I just tell him what he wants to hear.

"There will be others," he says, in a weak ass attempt to placate me. "What did you do with her body? I shouldn't have to ask this, but seeing as though what happened last time, I have to ask."

I suck back a malicious response. "It's taken care of."

I follow my new conquest to a small apartment community. I'm glad she doesn't have a gate. I'm even more glad to see that she lives on the first floor. Easy access. I wonder if she leaves her windows up all the time like Solanie used to do.

I remember I'm still on the phone with Nate when he starts laughing and carrying on about Solanie being dead, as if killing Solanie was an easy thing for me to do.

"I'll call you later." I hang up in his face.

I grit my teeth. Nate is starting to wear on my nerves. I'm already regretting choosing him over Solanie. Maybe it should have been him burnt to death in my house in the woods. Maybe then, I could still have my Solanie.

Ever since Daddy died, Nate has taken over his role in my life, expecting me to answer to him like I'm not a grown ass man. He always thought he was the smarter one, and I just fell back, allowing him to tell me what to do like I'm a child.

He got some nerve questioning how I killed Solanie and asking where I dumped the body. I've always been in charge of getting rid of the bodies. The more I think about it, I've always been in charge of doing the grimy shit. Meanwhile, he just gets to reap the high of the kill, reap the benefits of my hard work.

What was I thinking, killing the one thing that gave me any resemblance of peace? Regret makes me sick to my stomach, and there's only one way to soothe this stomachache.

Killing Nate.

KNIGHT

I haven't left Solanie's side since she was admitted to this hospital. It was by the grace of God we even found it. Deon was keeping Solanie so far in the boondocks that the nearest hospital was almost an hour away.

It took a lot out of me to leave her. To allow Ralph, one of the guys that came with me, to take her inside of the hospital. To pretend he'd ran across her in the middle of the street, needing help. As much as I didn't like the plan, I had to listen to reason. I couldn't walk into that hospital holding Solanie like I wanted to. There would be too many questions. How did I know where she was being kept? If I knew the identity of her captor, why hadn't I gone to the police?

It was just a lot easier to let Ralph carry her inside, pretending he'd found her. Pretending she'd escaped from that sick ass nigga Deon...

I thought I was going to lose her. I don't think I've ever been so scared in my life. Now, as I stare at her sleeping in this hospital bed, I can finally breathe easy knowing I'll never let her out of my sight again.

There's a price on Deon's head. I'm talking about the kind of money that would make a nigga snitch on his momma. So I know it won't be long before I get that call. I put out strict orders that he is to be taken alive. He is in no way to be killed. No, that's my job.

I don't take pleasure in ending anyone's life. I never have. That's why it's been years since someone died by my hands. I don't think I'll be able to answer to God about all the blood that is stained on my hands when the time comes.

But Deon, I think God fully understands why I have to send that nigga to hell.

Solanie stirs in her sleep, drawing my attention back to her beautiful face. The only part of her that is unmarred. Deon is one sick motherfucker, evident by all the scars, cuts and bruises that decorate Solanie's body. But he made sure he never touched her face.

I swear, I'm going to enjoy hearing him beg for his life.

Two knocks on the door draw my attention away from Solanie. I stand up when I see two uniformed cops. I hate that they even have to be involved. Solanie will get her justice, but not the kind of justice they have in mind.

"Let them do their jobs," Momma says before they fully enter the room. I swear that woman can read my mind.

After making it to this country ass hospital, Kian called Momma and Kurtis with an update. We all have a story planned, even though I know the cops will know we're full of shit. I really don't give a fuck though. If they were on their jobs, they would have found Solanie a long time ago. Way before she had to endure whatever that sick piece of shit put her through. Anger has its way with my body, and my fists clench in response to it.

A doctor enters the room after the police.

"I'm sorry, but we need to wake her," one of them says.

"Is that really necessary?" Momma asks, turning into that overprotective woman I recognize from childhood.

"I'm sorry. Excuse my manners. I'm Officer Pluton. I didn't catch your name?"

"Mrs. King," she says.

He looks around the room at all of us. "You're all family?"

"Yeah," I answer. "But her mother and stepfather are on their way as well."

He nods his head like he understands, but his face says something different. "I guess it's best we allow her to sleep. We've already notified Houston Police Department about Miss James' arrival. I believe they are sending some detectives who will need to question her."

I barely acknowledge that he's still talking, so him and his partner catch the hint and exit the room.

"When can she go back to Houston?" I ask the doctor, not wanting her to stay in this backwoods ass hospital longer than she has to. All of their equipment looks past outdated. She can't possibly get the medical attention she really needs here.

"Mr. King, I understand your eagerness to get your fiancée back home," he says.

Yeah, I told him Solanie was my fiancée. She will be sooner than later.

He continues speaking. "But with the extent of her injuries, it's best she stays put at least a week."

I huff.

"Miss James is in very bad shape. She's lost a lot of blood. She suffered some kind of blunt force trauma to her head. There are numerous cuts and lacerations all over her body. Some of the wounds look to be infected. She has two broken ribs, not to mention the stab wound in her stomach. It's a miracle she was found when she was, a minute or two later, and she wouldn't be alive right now." The doctor pauses and sighs, "I know this is probably going to be hard to hear, but there is also evidence that Miss James was violently raped… There's some tearing, and she has—"

"Alright!" I yell louder than I'd intended. The doctor doesn't look surprised by my reaction. I guess he knows if the roles were reversed and I was talking about his woman lying in this hospital bed, he'd react the same way.

He gives me a sympathetic look before leaving the room.

No one says another word for hours.

SOLANIE

He found me. He saved me. What my heart feels when I look at Knight makes the pain in my body almost disappear. He's smiling at me, even though there's pain in his eyes. It's easy to see that he blames himself.

"Solanie," he whispers as soon as I open my eyes. He reaches for my hand.

My mouth is so dry. A woman I instantly recognize from the portrait in his house walks to my side and bends a straw to my mouth.

"Solanie, this is my mother," Knight says.

"Hi, Solanie. I'm Ida. It's nice to finally meet you." Her voice is as sweet as honey and matches the smile on her face. "I've been waiting so long to meet you. I just hate that we're meeting under these circumstances."

I do too.

"I'll step out now and give you two some privacy."

"She's been here since you got here," Knight tells me. "I been trying to tell her to go home, but she ain't having it."

My heart swells. I already love his mother.

"You're safe now, Solanie. I promise you ain't ever gotta worry about nothing happening to you ever again. I put that on my life." He pats his chest as he speaks with passion.

"How did y-you find me?" I ask him.

"I put everything I had into finding you, Solanie. I'm sorry it took me so long." His eyes fall, but not before I see the guilt in them.

"And Deon? Is he dead?"

Knight's jaw flexes. "Not yet. But that muthafucka is on borrowed time, Solanie. I promise you. He won't be breathing for too much longer."

I'm shocked by Knight's words and the wrath I see on his face. All this time, I wondered what people saw in Knight that made them fearful. Now, I see it firsthand.

"You don't gotta be afraid of that nigga no more. He'll never come near you again."

I wish I could find safety in Knight's words, but I don't. He doesn't know the things I've been through. He hasn't seen evil so up close and personal like I have. I'm not sure I'll ever feel safe again.

"Solanie." Knight's voice is grave. His eyes were just as solemn. "I'm going to ask you to do something that might sound a lil' strange."

I'm afraid of what's about to come out of his mouth, but I also know I'll do whatever he asks.

"The cops will be here any minute, and they gonna have a million questions. Babe, I need you to tell them you escaped. I need you to tell them Ralph was driving down the street and saw you laying on the side of the road. I need you to tell them you have no idea who took you."

I gasp because I know where this is headed.

"I can't let the cops find Deon before I do." Knight's voice is desperate. "I can't, Solanie. I just can't."

"You're going to kill him?"

"Solanie..."

My heartbeat speeds up. "Have you ever killed anyone before, Knight?"

He closes his eyes like my question is causing him physical pain.

Finally, his reputation makes sense. Now I understand it all.

"You don't have to answer that," I quickly say. Relief washes over his face. "But promise me you won't show Deon no mercy."

I can't read his facial expression. It's a mixture of shock, regret, and anger. He nods and effortlessly changes the subject. "Your mom is here," he says with a smile. She just stepped out. She and your stepdad went down the street for some donuts or something."

Tears well in my eyes at the mention of my mother. There were so many times that I thought I'd never see her again. There's an urgency forming inside of me, needing to see her face now.

Knight swallows hard, questioning if he's said something wrong because my chest is now heaving. He starts talking so fast that it's kind of hard to catch everything he's saying. "Ya girls Candace and Mariah are on their way. They were so happy when they heard the news. They were sick as hell without you. It was hard on them... hard on all of us."

When I smile, it feels as if I'm erasing the pain in my heart. I'm about to be reunited with everyone that I love. It's all so overwhelming that it feels as if my heart will explode.

I'm tired and I want to sleep, but staring at Knight feels so good that I never want to close my eyes again.

Momma and Bryan burst into the room like a tornado. Momma rushes up to my bedside and grabs both of my hands. Tears are falling out of her eyes like a dam that's collapsed.

"My baby is alive! Oh, thank you Jesus! My baby is alive!"

She leans down to hug me, and I accept her embrace, ignoring the burn from the wound in my stomach. I never thought I'd hug my momma again, so I don't care about the pain in my body. I fold into her arms like I'm six years old again, and I can't tell her tears from my own.

I'm alive.

I survived.

Deon didn't win. Gratefulness floods out of me in the form of sobs.

Soon, my hospital room is full of love. Mariah, Candace and James, Ida is back, and of course Knight is still here. Two detectives from Houston show up. They're going to ask questions that I won't be able to answer truthfully. Lies I will have to tell in order to protect Deon from their capture so that he can meet an even worse fate with Knight.

And that's perfectly fine with me.

KNIGHT

The fucking Beauty Butcher?

I know I heard Solanie correctly, but it's still hard to believe what she's telling me. I'm trying to get as much information out of her as I can before this little time alone we have together is disturbed.

People have been in and out of her hospital room all day. I know she has so many people in her life that care about her, so I can't trip about them taking up so much of her time. But I've been dying for just a few minutes alone with her.

She blinks and winces as she tries to readjust herself in the small bed. "Yeah. He's The Beauty Butcher," she repeats. "And he has a brother. They're the ones that have been killing all those women."

Realization that she could have been next hits me like a bucket of cold water straight to the face. I can't believe I came so close to losing her at the hands of some lunatic ass niggas.

The police have been searching high and low for this serial killer, and now I have his identity. I'm going to do them and the city a favor by erasing his existence from the earth.

"His brother," I say quickly. "Tell me about him."

Solanie looks like it hurts to even try to remember anything about her time with Deon. She rattles off a few descriptions that won't help me much. I tell her to relax and run my hand across her head. I know I'll never know the extent of what she went through, but I can see hints of it by the way she flinches every time I touch her.

I'm going to make Deon regret the day he ever chose her.

Just as I thought, her room is full of people in a matter of minutes. Her parents, her friends, more cops asking more questions. I don't want to leave her side, but I need to find this nigga Deon. I won't be able to sleep until I put his ass to sleep.

I bend down to kiss Solanie on her cheek, telling her I'll be right back, then I slip out of her room.

There are reporters hanging outside of the hospital, hoping to catch a glimpse of the woman who'd been found after being missing for four weeks. I walk toward my car, hoping they don't notice me or that they at least have the good sense not to approach me with the dumb shit.

I'm in nowhere near the mood to have a microphone shoved in my face. I make it to my car unnoticed and leave the hospital parking lot. I dial Kian's number on my cell and wait impatiently for him to answer.

"'Sup?" he says.

"You won't believe this shit," I say.

"Uh oh."

"Where you at?"

"I'm actually headed out that way... with Mariah."

I'd be lying if I said I wasn't shocked to hear that. "You got Mariah with you?"

"Yeah," Kian says.

I chuckle. "Alright then, my nigga. I guess I'll sit here and wait for you to drop ya girlfriend off."

"Don't start that shit, Knight," he says.

I hang up, not knowing how I feel about Kian kicking it with Mariah. She's a good girl and the type of woman that he needs in his life, but I'm not so sure she can handle a nigga like my little brother. He still has a lot of growing up to do, and I ain't trying to have him hurt her 'cause that'll hurt Solanie.

And she's been hurt enough to last a lifetime.

Mariah gives me a shy smile before she walks off toward the entrance of the hospital. I look over at my brother, shooting him a warning with my eyes.

"Do you know what you're doing, nigga?"

He tries to brush my words off. "It ain't even like that."

"What's it like then?"

"We just chilling. Getting to know each other. She needs someone right now, and I'm just trying to be that shoulder, ya know?"

"Let me find out."

He laughs. "So what did you want to talk to me about?"

"Oh yeah!" I'd been thrown off by Kian and Mariah. "Get this. Solanie tells me that nigga Deon is the fuckin' Beauty Butcher."

"Shut the fuck up! You lying!"

I shake my head. "I wish I was."

I can see the wheels popping wheelies in Kian's head. A slow smile creeps upon his face. "So, after we kill this nigga, the city should give us a medal or the keys to the city or some shit like that, right?"

I would have laughed if Solanie wasn't laying up in a hospital bed with multiple injuries caused by that nigga's hand. If Solanie didn't flinch every time someone came close to her. If I didn't have this overwhelming, suffocating feeling of guilt knowing that nigga took her from *my* driveway. Even knowing that I'm going to fucking kill the nigga doesn't soothe any of this for me.

"What else?" Kian asks, noticing the somber expression on my face.

I tell him everything Solanie told me earlier. He nods and hangs on to my every word. "Oh, let's get ready to play," he says once I'm finally finished telling him everything I know.

"You ain't said nothing but a word," I say as we both get in my car and head back to the city.

SOLANIE

Every bone in my body cries in protest to what the doctor is saying. I've been here a little over a week, and she's telling me it's time for me to be discharged. I still feel pain every time I move. I still feel fear with every thought. How will I ever be able to go back into that world, especially knowing he's still out there?

Tears well in my eyes against my will. I don't want Momma to see me cry. I don't want her to know just how afraid I really am. I'm sure by now, Deon has learned that I'm still very much alive by the constant news coverage of my return. I'm so glad I'd listened to Knight and didn't tell the cops about Deon or the fact that he's The Beauty Butcher. The media coverage would have been so much worse.

No one knows what Deon is capable of. No one knows all of the things I had to endure under his captivity. If they did, there's no way they would allow me to leave this hospital away from the protection of the armed police officers that roam the halls.

Knight tells me he'll protect me, but that doesn't alleviate the suffocating fear that I feel. I could never tell him I don't feel safe with him. I could never crush his pride by reminding him that Deon was able to get to me at *his* house. The thought never leaves my mind, though I make sure it doesn't leave my mouth.

The doctor is going over the medications I'll have to take, telling Momma everything she'll need to know about the timeframe of my complete healing. Listening to her talk about my numerous injuries makes me realize the depths of Deon's depravity. He'd strangled me into unconsciousness on so many occasions that the doctors think I won't ever completely recover some of my memories from my time in his capture. For that, at least I'm thankful. The memories I do have are haunting enough. It's hard to close my eyes and not see his face.

"Is that what you want, Solanie?"

I look up and see Momma staring at me, concern all over her face. These weeks of me missing have terribly aged her, another reminder that Deon not only hurt me, but everyone connected to me.

"Uh, what?" I have no idea what she's talking about, but when I look around the room, I see everyone's eyes are on me, awaiting my response.

"I was just telling ya momma that you're going to be staying with me," Knight says. "I have the resources to hire an in-home nurse that can take care of everything you need."

I hope he can't read the expression on my face. I hope he can't tell that I'd rather stay anywhere than in his house. I don't want to return to the place where all of this started.

"You'll be safe there," Knight says, reading every doubt in my eyes. "I promise you'll be safe there, Solanie. I upgraded my security. Nobody can get a mile near my property without me knowing. I can get some security guards on site too. Whatever you need to feel safe." His voice and face are pleading with me to just say yes.

I look over at Momma who looks eased by the things Knight has just said. I can tell she feels that I'll be safer with him than with her. She has a confidence in his ability to protect me that I don't have.

"Uh, okay. Sure." I hear myself agreeing even though my mind is reeling.

In what feels like minutes, I'm being wheeled out of the hospital by Knight. Reporters are in my face before I can blink, begging for a soundbite they can play over and over on the news.

I don't want my face on the news. I don't want Deon to see how broken he made me.

I keep my head down as Knight and Kian yell obscenities at them until they finally get out of our way. I feel like I'm outside of my body as I'm being buckled inside of Knight's truck. I swallow the fear that's threatening to come out of me in the form of vomit as we head back to Houston.

Knight wasn't lying when he said he'd upgraded his security system. Cameras are mounted at every possible angle around his home's exterior. There's motion sensors everywhere that can pick up so much as a leaf blowing in the wind. There's no way a person could bypass entering the access code on the wrought iron gate surrounding his estate. There's even two obviously armed men standing outside the front door of Knight's house. They're just as tall and muscular as Knight, making me wonder if they're somehow related.

Knight pulls his car into the garage. He looks over at me before shutting off the engine. He pulls my hand inside of his, brings it up to his lips, and kisses it. "I promise that nigga ain't gonna be able to get near you here, Solanie."

After seeing all of this, I finally believe him.

The first thing I do once we're inside the house is get in Knight's oversized soaking tub. Most of my lacerations have healed well enough to be submerged in the warm water. I lie back and try to clear my head of my thoughts, which is harder to do than it should be. There's jazz music playing in the background, and I try to lose myself in the melody of the saxophone playing over the speakers.

Knight's light knocks precede his entrance into the bathroom. "It's me," he announces as if I'm not looking right at him. He sits on the corner of the tub and pours more bath salt into the warm water. "Is there anything I can get you? Are you hungry or something?"

I've been eating hospital food for the last week and a half, and before that, I was barely being fed. I've lost more weight than I'd ever thought was possible. Dark circles have found a home under my sunken eyes. I look terrible, but every time I catch Knight staring at me, it's like he's looking at the most beautiful woman in the world. My heart swells in my chest, and I don't know how I'd ever thought I would want to be anywhere but right here with this man.

The man that I dreamed about every single night I was locked in that room. The man whose face I'd try to conjure up every time Deon hurt me. The man who I knew would eventually find me.

My Knight.

"I could eat a steak and lobster, potatoes, fried shrimp, chicken tenders, cheddar biscuits, and some iced tea," I tell him.

He looks like he doesn't know if I'm being serious or not. I laugh and reach my hand out to rub the side of his face. It feels like a dream that I'm really here with him, that I'm actually touching him. Even though my body has been abused in every way possible, it yearns to be touched by him.

"I'm sorry, Solanie," he says.

I'm frozen at his words.

"I should have never let that nigga get close enough to touch you."

"Shhh." I try to silence his guilt by placing my lips on top of his.

He closes his eyes and I pull him closer to me. His kiss is gentle, and I can tell he's holding back, afraid of hurting me.

He stands up and peels his clothes from his body. He climbs into the tub behind me, takes the sponge from my hand and starts washing my body as if he's trying to wash away every bruise, every hurt, and every memory.

KNIGHT

I keep my arms around Solanie throughout the night. She keeps waking up, screaming and panting in fear. I feel powerless not knowing what to do to make things right.

"It's me. It's Knight," I tell her. "I'm here, Solanie,"

She falls back asleep, only to wake right back up a couple of hours later. This happened all night, and now that it's morning, I climb out of bed, trying not to wake her because she needs some kind of sleep. I'm used to working off of two to three hours because it's all I've done since she went missing.

I close the bedroom door quietly after leaving her a note letting her know I'll be in my office if she needs me. I don't know what I expected when Solanie came back, but it definitely wasn't this broken shell of a woman that I once knew.

Deon may not have been able to kill her physically, but he succeeded in killing who she once was. The light has long gone out of her eyes and been replaced with fear. I would do anything in my power to erase everything that nigga did to her, or at least erase the memories. I never in my life thought it would be possible to hate someone as much as I hate his ass.

I get to the front door before Cindy, the in-home healthcare nurse I'd hired, is able to ring the doorbell and wake Solanie up. She's smiling at me and has a lot of equipment with her. I'm not sure if Solanie needs all of this, but I'll spare no expense to help her heal faster.

"Who are these guys?" She nervously looks over at the

security guards I'd hired to make Solanie feel safe. I didn't really need them, but I saw how Solanie visibly relaxed once she saw them. I ain't gonna lie; it made me feel some type of way to know it took seeing them for her to feel safe here with me.

"Security," I answer, and I invite her inside. I wonder why she chose to wear her scrubs so tight. She does have the kind of body that would make a nigga want to hand over his credit card, but the only thing on my mind are the scars all over Solanie's body.

"Where should I set up?"

I lead her to the spare bedroom down the hall where she takes out a lot of shit that I know Solanie doesn't need.

"She's sleeping right now," I tell her.

"Oh, that's fine. I'll be here when she gets up."

I leave her in the bedroom and walk into my kitchen. I don't know what the hell I'm doing in the kitchen, but I try to whip up something that resembles a breakfast. My chef is usually here by now, but I gave him the day off.

I can hear my bedroom door opening. I turn around with a skillet in one hand and a spatula in the other.

Solanie is wiping her eyes and yawning. "You let me sleep in?"

"I figured you could use the extra rest."

"I'm sorry I kept you up all night."

I frown at her. "You ain't gotta apologize for that." It's not her fault she's still having nightmares about the shit that nigga did to her.

She looks at her hands like she doesn't know what to do with them. "You're cooking?" She squints her eyes.

"I was trying." I look down at my struggle eggs. They look pitiful, and I can't believe I don't even know how to make eggs.

“Your nurse is here,” I tell her.

“Oh,” she says.

I call Cindy, and she introduces herself to Solanie before taking her blood pressure and checking her stomach wound. She gives Solanie some antibiotics that are supposed to prevent infection in the stab wound that had been inches away from a major artery.

“How do you feel?” Cindy asks her.

“Better,” Solanie says.

“You’ll get there. It’s a process but your body knows what it’s doing. It’ll heal in its own time,” Cindy says.

By the time they finish talking, I’ve dumped the eggs and burnt toast in the trash. “You wanna go get some breakfast somewhere?” I ask Solanie.

She laughs at me, but then her voice goes dejected. “I don’t really have an appetite or anything.”

I don’t want to say anything about her thin frame, but she needs to eat. It’s obvious that nigga was starving her, but I don’t want to push the issue, making her think she’s anything but beautiful in my eyes.

“Try to eat something. Even if it’s just a couple of bites of toast, especially with all the medications you’re taking,” Cindy advises. She looks Solanie over one more time before leaving. She leaves us her cell number, telling us to call her if anything changes suddenly with Solanie’s physical condition.

“You want some coffee or orange juice then?” I ask, walking toward the refrigerator.

“I’ll take some juice.” She sits on one of the bar stools and places her chin in the palm of her hand. Her eyes are looking off, and I can tell her mind is no longer here with me.

I pour the orange juice and place the cup in front of her. She jumps at the sound of the glass being set in front of her, a sound that would normally go unnoticed but must sound like a thunderstorm to Solanie. She blinks repeatedly like she's trying to bring her mind back to the present. She looks up at me, and her eyes are wet with tears. "I'm sorry, Knight. I don't know how you're going to be able to put up with this... with me."

I'm across the room and by her side within seconds. I pull her body close to mine, trying to comfort her before the tears have the chance to fall.

"I'm so fucked up now. I don't know if I'll ever be normal again," she cries. She buries her face in my chest, and my shirt goes wet with her tears. "I will totally understand if this is too much for you. Me waking up all during the night screaming and shit. And now I'm jumping at a glass of orange juice. It's cool if you can't do this and need to walk away. I swear I won't hold it against you."

"Solanie," I say slowly so she can understand everything that's about to leave my mouth. "I ain't going nowhere. I'ma be right here by your side, walking you through this. Just tell me what you need. Tell me how I can help you. You need to go talk to somebody, a psychologist or something? Just let me know, and I'll find the best one in Houston."

She trembles and breaks down in my arms. She's so tiny, so fragile, that I'm afraid if I hold on too tight, she'll shatter.

"Tell me what to do, Solanie," I plead with her. "Tell me what you need me to do to help you."

Her sobs are excruciating to me. Worse than any physical pain I've ever felt. I feel handicapped at not knowing what to do to help her. She pulls away from me and falls onto the floor. I've never seen anyone cry so hard. I wish I could take her pain and bear it myself if for one second it meant she didn't have to feel it. I wish I could pick up all the broken pieces of her, even if I cut myself in the process, and put her back together again.

"I just want the memories to stop," she says. "I just want to be able to close my eyes and not see him." She looks up at me, her eyes begging me to be able to make that happen.

I wring my hands to stop an itch to punch a wall. I never felt so powerless in my fucking life. I do the only thing I know how. I get on the floor with her, wrap my arms around her small frame, and hold her until the tears stop coming.

DEON

Solanie is alive.

Every local news channel ran the story until it was beat into the ground. On top of that, my face is plastered all over the TV as being a "person of interest" in The Beauty Butcher murders. The footage is fuzzy at best, but still, *I* know it's me. I haven't heard from Nate since all of this shit hit the fan, which is good. I don't need him calling for me to realize I've fucked up.

I need to get out of town. I know better than to go near my apartment. It's not the cops I'm worried about. They still don't know my identity, but by now, I'm sure Knight knows exactly who I am.

I would do anything to know just how the fuck Solanie survived that stab wound, let alone made it out of a burning house. The news is saying some bullshit about a man finding her on the side of the road clinging to life. I don't believe that for a minute because there is no way in hell some random man was traveling down that dirt road. For as long as I stayed out there working on that house, I never once saw one person drive by.

Ever.

Whoever found Solanie was on that side of town for one reason: They were looking for Solanie.

Which further lets me know Knight has been on to me for a minute now since he knew exactly where to find her. I know enough about him and his family to know right now there's a price on my head.

He'll have to find me first.

I ignore the building rage inside of me at the thought of him and Solanie laying up somewhere together. Him fucking every memory of me out of her. I only have myself to blame. I should have killed Knight a long time ago, way before he was ever able to uncover my identity. How the hell he was able to do so in the first place is beyond me. I can't worry about that though. I have to get the fuck outta dodge!

If the police are putting shit together to the point they have footage of me, then it won't be long before they're able to close in on me. Nate will do whatever it takes not to go down with me. He's probably somewhere right now plotting on a way to kill me.

That fucking Solanie! I should have put a bullet in her heart instead of a knife in her gut.

I ditch my car in a mall parking lot. My head is on a swivel, looking for anyone who could be lurking, waiting for the chance to ambush my ass. It's not funny how the hunter has now become the hunted.

I scan the parking lot for a car that will be easy to steal. First, I have to stop by Daddy's grave. A part of me is glad that I can only talk to him at a cemetery. I'm glad I don't have to see the look on his face knowing how bad I done messed up this time. He never made these kinds of mistakes. He never took women who had powerful boyfriends that could have him executed on sight for the right price.

Now I understand why he only took prostitutes.

I need to stop by his grave and explain myself. It'll be the last time I ever see his grave because once I'm gone, I won't ever step foot back in this city. I won't be able to until Knight King is dead. But even then, it probably won't be safe for me.

I'm trying to think straight and fast, but it's hard when I have so much shit on my mind, and I'm only working off two hours of sleep. Not to mention the fact I have to keep looking over my shoulder. I know I have enough money to run off to Mexico, but I need time to sit and research so I can find a country that doesn't extradite. Just because the police don't know who I am now, doesn't mean it'll stay that way.

I hop in a red Nissan Versa and drive off after taking two minutes to get it started. I make sure to obey all traffic laws, not wanting to draw any kind of attention to me riding in a stolen car. I probably have an hour or so before it's reported stolen. By then, I'll be long gone.

I should be hopping on I-45 and heading North, but I can't leave Houston without saying bye to Daddy. Against any second thoughts, I head toward the Morris Field Cemetery.

The sun is setting as I arrive. I find Daddy's grave without much effort. I've been here so many times that I could find it blindfolded.

"Daddy," I say as I stand over his tombstone. I read the familiar inscription describing him as a great man, husband, and father. It couldn't be any further from the truth. This cemetery is probably full of his victims to attest to that.

I stare down at the grave, knowing this will be the last time I'm ever able to visit him. I let out a deep breath and rub my hand over my fuzzy cheek. "I fucked up. Real bad this time."

"Shit, who you telling?"

I turn around to find Nate standing behind me. How the hell was he able to sneak up on me like that. I'm relieved to see it's him and not one of Knight's henchmen, but that relief doesn't last long. He's probably here to kill me, too.

"Nate, man, I..."

"I knew you was gonna fuck up, but I never imagined it would be this bad!" He's yelling, and spit is flying out of his mouth.

"They don't know anything. They just have a fuzzy ass video of me buying shoes that I been got rid of. That could be anybody in that video," I protest, while my eyes are searching the cemetery for somebody, anybody. As long as there is at least one other person here, Nate won't kill me. He's too smart to leave a witness.

"It's only a matter of time before that video leads to you, and when it does, it'll lead straight to me." Nate sounds defeated. "And if it doesn't, we still have to worry about that bitch talking. You broke the number one rule, Deon. You left a witness alive to tell."

"I thought she was dead. I stuck a fucking knife right through her! I even set the fuckin' house on fire, Nate. There's no reason she should have survived that."

"But she did, Deon. She did fuckin' survive. It's only a matter of time before she tells the cops everything about us."

I shake my head. "If she was gonna do that, she would have done it by now. She ain't going to the cops. Knight won't let her."

Nate laughs bitterly. "So I guess that's better? Instead of having the laws on our asses, we gotta worry about Knight King!"

"His beef ain't with you. It's with me." I point to my chest. "You ain't gotta worry about him. He doesn't know nothin' about you. I know he probably gonna end up killing me, and that's my bad for fucking up so bad."

"Killing you is like killing me." Nate drops his eyes. "We gotta try to get him before he can get to us."

My brother always has been better than me at everything. Just days ago, I was plotting on his death. Here he is, ready to go toe-to-toe with a man who owns the city, behind my mistake.

"How do you figure we do that?"

He sighs. “I don’t know, Deon. I need some time to plan it. This ain’t no ordinary target.”

“I don’t have that much time. I know that nigga has a bounty on my head by now.”

Nate reaches in his coat pocket and tosses me a thick white envelope. “Yeah, he probably does. Take that and get the fuck out the city. Go lay low somewhere until I can figure some things out. Don’t call me under any circumstances. I’ll reach out to you if I need to.”

I look at the envelope in my hands, trying to eyeball the amount. Then I try to read Nate’s expression, but he’s avoiding all eye contact with me.

He walks up to me, hugs me, and then turns his back on me as he walks away.

I ignore the voice in the back of my head telling me I’ll never see my brother again.

SOLANIE

Knight is wearing all black and a facial expression that I've never seen before. It scares me, and it doesn't take a mind reader to be able to tell he's up to no good.

"I gotta make a run," he says, avoiding my eye contact. "I'll be back in a couple of hours. If you need me, hit me on my cell. Tim and Bo will still be outside, so you don't have to worry about anything."

"Where are you going, Knight?"

He turns his back to me, not wanting to lie to my face.

"Knight?"

"Don't make me lie to you, Solanie. You've got enough on your mental right now to be worried about the shit I got going on."

I sit straight up in the bed. Something is not right. I feel it in the center of my very being. "Knight, please."

He turns around to face me and he's scowling. "I'm going to kill that muthafucka, Solanie!" His voice doesn't match the anger on his face. He sounds strained, pained, and tortured. He slaps his chest. "As a man, I have to do this! I have to make things right."

He drops his head and I climb onto my knees in the bed, reaching out for him. He falls into my arms. I take several deep breaths to settle the emotions racing through me.

"Take me with you."

Knight pulls away from me. "What?"

"Take me with you."

He's shaking his head. "I can't do that, Solanie. You done been through enough. You don't need to see this muthafucka ever again in your life."

"But I do, Knight! I do need to see him again! I need to see the life drain from his eyes to ever feel safe again. You don't know how many days I plotted that bastard's death! Every time he climbed on top of me, raped me, I imagined the day I would kill him. Every time he beat me until I blacked out, I thought about this moment right here." I stop to catch my breath. "The moment I'd be able to kill his ass."

Knight is staring at me. Every word I just tossed at him was like a dagger in his chest, so I pull him closer to me to stop the bleeding. He kisses the top of my head, and in an almost inaudible whisper, he says, "Go get dressed."

I don't ask Knight if he's done this before. I can see it in his eyes. I'm not sure how I feel about that, so I decide not to think about it. Not when we're so close to Deon. Adrenaline pulses through my veins, knowing I'm about to take back everything that he stole from me.

"You sure that nigga in here?" Knight turns around and asks Kian.

"Yep. Nigga checked in about an hour ago."

There's something about Kian that I can't put my finger on. I know Mariah is in over her head with him because there's a dangerous edge to him that scares the shit out of me.

"Nigga stupid as hell," Knight says. "Shoulda been long gone by now."

"Maybe he doesn't know anyone is looking for him," I offer.

"He knows who he fucked with when he took you," Kian says. "He shoulda been on the first thing smoking out the country, or at least out the state."

If Kian is right, Deon is laid up in this ran down looking motel, without a care in the world. Just like I'd been the night he took me from outside Knight's house.

I follow Knight and Kian as they walk to the front desk of the motel. A girl with a cheap blue wig smiles at both of them as soon as they step up to her desk. She runs her tongue across her teeth and grins at Kian. "Hey, zaddy."

"What up, Monica?" Kian says. "You got them keys?"

Her smile gets bigger as she reaches behind her and retrieves a set of keys. "I turned off all the cameras like you asked me, too."

Kian smirks and opens his hand for her to drop the keys.

"You promise you gonna come see me tomorrow, right?" She wants to know before she drops the keys into Kian's open palm.

Kian doesn't miss a beat. "I told you, I'ma wear that pussy out, girl."

She squeals and gives him the keys. I'm not sure what the hell just happened, but I follow Knight and Kian back to the car.

"Wait here, Solanie."

I frown. "Why?"

Knight takes a deep breath. "Solanie, we going in here to get the nigga. I promise we ain't gonna do shit without you. Trust me, okay?"

I stare into his eyes, and I can't find a lie, so I get back inside the Suburban. I cross my arms across my chest and watch him and Kian as they use the key Monica just gave them to slip into Deon's hotel room.

FBI SPECIAL AGENT TAYLOR

I hang up with Detective Hardee and literally run to my car. He has a girl in his office right now who claims she recognizes the man from the shoe store surveillance tapes.

I make it to the police station in record time. As soon as I walk into Detective Hardee's office, I'm taken off guard by the appearance of the woman sitting across from him. She has burn scars all over her arms, hands, and neck. Her eyes are jumpy and nervous.

"Hello, I'm Agent Taylor." I offer her a warm smile, hoping to ease some of her nerves.

Her voice is timid. "Hi, I'm Brittany."

"Brittany was just telling me she thinks she recognizes the man from the shoe store tapes," Detective Hardee says.

Brittany's eyes are on her hands. She keeps folding and unfolding them.

"Oh yeah?" I ask.

She nods, takes a deep breath, and I can tell that whatever is about to come out of her mouth is going to be hard for her. "You know that app Swipe or Like?" She looks up at me, and I nod, encouraging her to continue. "Well, one night after me and my man got into it, I went on there. I was pissed off and looking to do some revenge cheating. If I woulda known what I was getting myself into, I woulda never downloaded that fucking app!"

Fat tears chase one another down her cheeks. She wipes them away with the back of her hand and continues speaking. “There was a dude who had liked my picture, and I thought he was kinda cute, so I liked his picture back. We got to private messaging, and I liked his vibe, so I invited him to come through. I know, I know.” She holds her hand in the air as if Hardee or I was about to lecture her on her unwise decision. “It was stupid as hell. Fast forward a lil’ bit, and when the dude arrives, he doesn’t look shit like his profile picture. At first, I was pissed about it, but like I said, I was just trying to do some revenge cheating, so I was like fuck it. We talked for a lil’ bit, and he seemed cool, but as soon as we got to my bedroom, he flipped out on me.”

She pauses, and it looks like she’s about to start hyperventilating. I get up and stand next to her. I rub her back, trying to comfort her in whatever way I can. I can tell by the look in her eyes she’s retelling the worst night of her life. Hardee slides a few tissues across his desk, and I hand them to Brittany.

“He forced me to suck his—perform oral sex on him. Then, he beat me up like real bad. Every time I thought he was about to stop hitting me, he started right back up again. He raped me… like three or four times. Honestly, I lost count. It was horrible. I was in so much pain, and I just didn’t want it to hurt no more, so I just laid there and gave up. Eventually, he had enough and left. Or so I thought he was leaving, but what he was really doing was setting my apartment on fire!”

I look up at Hardee, and he has a look on his face that matches how I’m feeling. I’m not sure if The Beauty Butcher is behind what happened to Brittany, but whoever is responsible deserves to pay.

She’s full out bawling now. The tissues crumpled tightly in her hands. I kneel down in front of her and take both of her hands in mine. I’ve never been a nurturer, but I can’t just stand here and watch this woman break down in front of me and do nothing.

"I could smell the fire, but it's like my mind couldn't wrap around the fact my apartment was burning up!" Brittany swipes the tears from her eyes, but they just keep coming. "I was in so much pain, and I just wanted to lay there and die, but then I thought about my babies. I got three kids, and I just thank God they were at my sister's house that night. I don't know where I pulled the strength from, but I pulled it from somewhere. I got myself up from that bed, even though every part of my body was hurting so bad. All I kept thinkin' is I can't let my babies grow up without me. I can't let my babies grow up without me. I made it to my balcony and the fire department was already there. They put a ladder up against the balcony, and I climbed down it. I guess I was lookin' real bad 'cause everybody was talkin' 'bout how I needed to get to the hospital fast."

"Brittany, did you tell anyone at the hospital about the rape?" I damn near have my fingers crossed. DNA is the police lottery.

She shakes her head.

My shoulders drop.

"Y'all don't understand. This nigga was crazy! I knew if I told anybody about the rape, they'd find him, but not before he found me and finished what he started."

"And you think the man that attacked you that night is the same man from our tapes?"

Brittany inhales and lets out a rush of air. "When I seen that video on the news, I knew immediately it was Ben. For as long as I live, I'll never forget that man's face. I see it every time I close my eyes. Knowing he was the fuckin' Beauty Butcher, I just couldn't stay silent no more. He's killed so many women... I could have been one of them."

"Ben?" I stand up and look over at Hardee.

"That's what he said his name was," Brittany says. She pulls out her phone and shows us a screenshot image of Ben's

Swipe or Like dating profile. "This isn't how he really looks though, so his name probably ain't really Ben."

"Pull up that website," I tell Hardee. His fingers get to typing at lightning speed on his computer. "See if that profile is still there." It's a long shot but still worth a shot.

My eyes fall back to the broken woman before me. Her attack was brutal, and she's lucky to be alive, but her attack isn't The Beauty Butcher's usual M.O. Regardless, she deserves justice, and I'm going to personally make sure she gets it. I add her to the growing list of cases that are stacking on top of one another on my back.

"Son of a bitch!" Hardee shouts. "Profile no longer exists."

I look over at Brittany and ask, "Is there anything you can remember about him that you think could possibly help us ID the guy that attacked you?"

She's silent for a while and then she says, "It coulda all been a lie, but he did say he worked for the Mull Brothers. He said he was their construction manager."

Hardee is already pulling up the contact info for the popular home builder. He's on the phone with them just as fast.

"We're gonna get the man that attacked you, Brittany, whether he worked for them or not. Let me tell you something about me. I've solved every single case that has ever crossed my desk." I ignore the nagging reminder that Knight King threatens to ruin my perfect record. "And your case won't be any different. I give you my word on that."

She manages to smile through her tears.

Hardee slams his phone down. "They had a construction manager who recently just up and quit. Black guy, medium build. Could be our Butcher."

Hardee is already on his feet and calling someone over to take the rest of Brittany's statement. We damn near run out the door. We need to get to the Mull Brother's corporate office and get every single detail on the identity of the construction manager who used to work for them.

I don't believe in coincidences.

DEON

I know I'm not tripping. It sounds like the door to my room is being opened. I'm half sleep, so I could be dreaming. I roll over on my back, and when I open my eyes, I could laugh at the irony of two figures dressed in black standing over me.

"Wake up, motherfucka."

So this is it. This is how I'll meet my end. I only have myself to blame. I should have taken that money Nate gave me and got the fuck out of dodge. I should have never given Knight the chance to find me. How he tracked me down in this seedy motel is beyond me, but yet he's here.

Things are coming full circle, I guess. So many nights, Nate and I crept inside the bedrooms of the unsuspecting sleeping occupants; now the tables have turned.

I'm yanked out of the bed and tossed on the floor. I'm being stomped on, and I can't even fight back. The force behind the kicks are so strong that I swear I can feel a couple of my ribs shattering. At this rate, my spleen will be next. I try to cover my head with my arms and hands. The kicking goes on for what feels like forever. I can taste blood, my blood. Every part of my body hurts so bad that I can't pinpoint which part hurts the worst.

"Get that nigga up!" Knight yells.

I know I'm about to pass out, and I welcome the reprieve from the beating. I can't keep my eyes open. I keep going in and out.

I'm being shoved against a wall. I try to keep my eyes open

because I want to see what Knight is about to do to me, but my eyelids feel like bricks, and I just want to go to sleep.

"Look at me, bitch," Knight sneers.

My eyes are so heavy...

Whack! His fists connect with the side of my face. I hear the bones in my jaw crack, and then the pain shoots up through my head like I've just been hit upside the head with a sledgehammer.

"I said look at me, bitch."

I couldn't look at him if I tried. My head hangs low, and my legs feel like overcooked noodles.

Whack! Whack!

Lights out.

And I'm grateful for that.

I don't know how long I was out, but it sucks to be awake again. I look around and see I'm lying on the floor of my motel room. I start coughing up blood. It's hard to breathe. I'm wheezing just to get enough air in my lungs. I'm sure I have some kind of internal bleeding, or my lungs could be about to collapse.

Kian yanks me up my feet. I can barely stand. My feet are wobbly and unsteady. I feel like I weigh a thousand pounds.

"Let's go for a lil' ride, bitch," Kian says as he pushes me out the door.

I wonder how much they paid the hotel attendant for a key to my room. I wonder how the hell they even knew I was here. None of this matters though, because I won't live to find out any of the answers.

Once we make it to their vehicle, I'm thrown into the back. "Arrgh!" Shit hurts like hell, but at least the beating has stopped. I shut my eyes just as the doors slam. I haven't ever gotten my ass beat this bad before. It hurts just to breathe! Both of my eyes are almost swollen shut, and my vision is blurry and hazy.

Damn, I really fucked up this time. Why the hell did I stay here? I should have been across the country by now! Stupid ass rookie mistake. I knew better. I knew Knight had eyes all over the city looking for me. I should have taken the money Nate gave me and got the fuck outta dodge. I figured choosing this raggedy ass motel and getting a couple of hours of sleep wouldn't hurt. I'd planned on sleeping just for a little bit before hitting the road. Now, that one little decision has cost me my life.

I hear the car starting, but I don't bother opening my eyes to see who's driving. It doesn't matter because someone is driving me to death's door. All I can do is hope that it's quick. Karma lets me know it won't be though. I've never showed any of my victims that kind of mercy, so I know it won't be shown to me.

"Can't say it's nice to see you again, Deon."

No matter how much it hurts, my head snaps up. Well damn, I wasn't expecting her to be here.

Solanie.

Still beautiful as ever, even with that ugly ass smirk on her face. Well, I'll be damned. This is really an unexpected twist.

How the tables have turned.

FBI SPECIAL AGENT TAYLOR

The Mull Brothers wouldn't release any information to us without a warrant, so we had to wait an entire hour for a judge to grant us one.

Now, we've finally been handed the employee file of a man named Deon.

I stare at the picture of our suspect's employee badge. He's a young black man, possible late twenties, just as the FBI profiler said he'd be. He could very well be the man from our shoe store surveillance.

I shove a still shot photo from the footage in one of the Mull Brothers' faces. "Is this the same guy that worked for you the last six years?"

He squints his eyes then shrugs. "It could be Deon. I can't really tell."

"Give me his last known address from his employee file," I demand. He's typing, and time seems to stand still before he finally looks up from his computer and gives us the address.

Google lets me know the address is an apartment community in an area of Houston that is prone to high crime. I enter the address in my phone's GPS, and Hardee and I are on our way there. I'm glad we're in his squad car instead of mine because he has sirens, and everybody gets the fuck out of the way as soon as we turn them on.

We make it to the apartment community in no time and head straight to apartment 902. We could knock, but we want to take this motherfucker by surprise. With our weapons drawn, Hardee kicks in the door.

I get a familiar burst of adrenaline that usually accompanies the feeling of closing in on a suspect. "Police!" I bellow as soon as we enter the small apartment.

My body is on a swivel as I scan the living area searching for any sudden movement. Hardee is on my heels, and we move in unison throughout the small apartment.

It's then I realize I'm not wearing a bulletproof vest. An onslaught of alarm causes sweat to run down my neck and back. If this guy really is The Beauty Butcher, he'll be armed, and I'll most definitely need that vest.

"Clear!" I call out as we leave the living area and walk down a short hallway to a bathroom. I ease the door open with a painful slowness, halfway expecting to receive bullets straight to my face.

Empty.

I have to force myself to breathe as we enter the bedroom. My hands have gone so sweaty that I'm afraid my Glock will slip right out of my hand. I try to calm my nerves, but knowing I could possibly be walking into a trap makes that a hard thing to do.

The bedroom is clear. We check the bedroom closet, and no one's there as well. A gush of relief rushes out of me. Now that I'm sure we're alone, I start looking through the place. It's easy to tell that our suspect had packed in a hurry before leaving.

We leave the apartment and question a few of the neighbors, but nobody wants to talk or be seen talking to us. I answer my ringing cell as we walk back to Hardee's squad car. It's our forensic scientist.

"Hey, Carol."

"Hey, Taylor. Uh, are you sitting down?"

"I am now," I say. "What's up?"

"Remember you asked me to look into a few of those cold cases?"

Oh, shit. I'd totally forgotten. "Yeah."

"Well, there was untested DNA in one of the evidence folders of Rochelle Jamison. As you know, DNA wasn't nearly as advanced back then as it is now... I ran the sample, and I got a match."

I'm hanging on waiting for Carol to spit it out, not sure why she's pausing for dramatic effect. "And?"

"And you'll never believe who the sample matched with."

"Who?" I ask.

SOLANIE

Deon is butt naked, tied to a chair in the middle of a warehouse. Kian says we can do whatever we want to Deon, and no one will hear his screams. I don't bother asking how he knows this. The blood stains on the floor let me know Deon won't be the first person to meet his end here.

My hands are trembling, and I'm wondering if I have it in me to really kill someone. Will I be able to look myself in the mirror knowing I'm the reason someone took their final breath? Then, I remember the days Deon made me do unspeakable things for a bottle of water. A new determination to see him bleed erases all doubt.

"You ready, babe?" Knight asks me. There's concern on his face. He's worried about me, thinking I shouldn't be here, that I should just let him handle it. I appreciate the concern he has for me, but I need to be the one to do this. I need to replace the memories of Deon hurting me with the memory of me killing him.

He's already looking pretty messed up. His eyes are almost swollen shut. The side of his mouth is bloody and sagging open. His breathing is labored. I could walk out of here right now, and he'd probably not even make it through the night.

Knight hands me a blow torch, his eyes still questioning if I want to do this.

Deon doesn't react to the tool in my hands. He can barely keep his eyes open. I wonder if he'll even feel anything. I press the trigger and watch the flames shoot out. My eyes go from Knight to Kian, both of them nodding, telling me to proceed.

I walk up to Deon.

"You ruined my life."

His chest is heaving up and down so slowly, I wonder if he's about to stop breathing. He starts coughing, blood shooting out of his swollen mouth. It takes a second for me to realize he's laughing.

He's actually fucking laughing.

He's sick.

I press the trigger on the blow touch and let the flame hit his bare chest. His laughter turns to hollowed screams. The smell of burning flesh is disgusting. I almost gag.

I pull the blow torch away, and now Deon's chest is rising and falling so fast, it looks like he's having a seizure.

"Solanie. This ain't you," he struggles to say.

"Fuck you! You don't know nothing about who I am!" I press the trigger on the blow touch and bring it back to his chest. Most of his flesh has peeled away.

I stare at the thing that tortured me for a month. The thing that violently ripped inside of my womb, no matter how hard it tried to reject him. I don't look at Knight, or Kian. This is between Deon and me.

I turn the blow torch on his dick. I am numb to his screams, numb to the smell, numb to everything but the desire of burning his dick completely off his body. He will never hurt me again. He will never be able to hurt anyone again with this thing.

I drop the torch to the floor. I didn't even realize I was crying until I taste the salty liquid on my lips. I stare at Deon, all burned and beat up, tied to the chair. He's pathetic. Nothing I do to him will compare to the hurt he's inflicted on so many families of the women he'd ripped out of their lives. Even death is too kind for him.

"You finished?" Knight wants to know. He walks up to me and wraps his arms around my trembling body. "You ready to finish this nigga off?"

"Wait." I want him to sit here and endure whatever pain he's feeling for a little longer.

"Nigga probably 'bout to die." Kian's face is disappointed. "He lucky I didn't get the chance to play with 'em."

All of our eyes are locked on Deon. I think he's gone into shock or something. He's trembling, moaning… dying.

I watch him suffer. I wait and wait, hoping each minute is worse than the one before. Finally, he's getting what he deserves. I'm so glad I listened to Knight. That I didn't let the cops get him. There's no way their punishment for him could ever be this gratifying. A lifetime in a cell would be a gift. No, he deserves every second of this.

It feels so satisfying seeing him so terrified. Now, he gets to know exactly how every woman he's killed felt. He used to talk about how much my fear turned him on. Now, I'm basking in his.

Knight hands me a pistol. "Let's get this over with."

I've never shot a gun in my life, but I cock it and aim it like a pro. I wait a few more seconds, not wanting to put Deon out his misery just yet.

"Look at me," I demand.

He struggles to lift his head, struggles even harder to open his eyes.

"There's consequences to disobedience, Deon."

Our eyes lock. I pull the trigger.

And just like that, the world becomes a better place.

FBI SPECIAL AGENT TAYLOR

Wait. What?

She repeats the name, but it still doesn't make sense to me.

"I need to get back to the station," I tell Hardee. I can't tell him what Carol has just revealed to me. Not until I get to the bottom of it myself.

Once we're back at the station, I hop out of Hardee's car without even saying goodbye to him. I get back to the FBI headquarters in record timing.

I make a beeline to my desk. The first thing I do is enter the name Carol gave into the FBI's name check database. His name is a common one, so my computer lags as it searches the entire fifty states for information.

"Come on." I drum my fingers on my desk, anxious for whatever the computer is about to reveal.

Finally, the screen stops loading, and I'm presented with forty-three different names. I narrow them down to the Houston area until I'm left with the person I'm looking for. I click on it and wait as his entire family genealogy loads.

Gregory Mitchell.

Late police captain Gregory Mitchell's DNA matches what was found on Rochelle Jamison. I can't wrap my mind around it.

There has to be some kind of mistake because if Captain Mitchell is responsible for all the prostitution murders, that means his sons would be The Beauty Butchers. But he only has one son…

Special Agent Nate Mitchell.

And Mitchell doesn't have a brother… that I've ever met.

I google a photo of Captain Mitchell and text it to Chandie, asking if he is the man she remembers seeing Rochelle get in the car with all these years ago.

I already know what her response will be.

Yes! That's the creepy looking motherfucker!

I click on Gregory Mitchell's family genealogy. It loads at the speed of a snail, but once it's finished, the facts can no longer be doubted.

Deon Mitchell *is* the younger brother of FBI Agent Nate Mitchell.

SOLANIE

I don't know how we made it back to Knight's. I don't know where Kian is or what's happened to Deon's body. Everything is a blur. The only thing I do know, is I'll never be the same again.

Ever.

Knight dismisses the men standing guard outside his house. We enter his house like zombies. He's leading me to the bathroom.

I can still smell the scent of burning flesh. I'm sticky with sweat and blood. Deon's blood. I feel dirty and disgusting, yet I also feel cleansed.

Knight is undressing me, pulling the sticky clothing from my body. I'm crying, but the tears aren't from sadness. I stare into Knight's eyes. They're heavy with an emotion that I can't read.

He's so beautiful, standing before me, undressing me so gently. There's blood on his skin, blood on his clothes.

I'm standing in just my bra and an expensive pair of black jeans that I know I'll never wear again.

Knight unbuttons the jeans, then unzips them. He slides them down my thighs. "Step outta them, Solanie."

I do as he's told me. My lacy underwear follows the jeans, and I step out of them too. When he stands back up, he unclasps my bra. He runs his finger across my cheek. I notice his knuckles are swollen, and some of his skin looks to have been peeled off.

I'm hit with a vision of Deon's chest with most of the flesh burnt off.

I shiver as a wave of repulsion rushes down my spine. I can still feel him, still smell him. His blood is on me. Pieces of his brain matter in my hair. I start to spaz out, needing every remnant of him off me.

Knight turns the shower on with one hand while his other arm is wrapped around me. "It's okay, Solanie. I'm gonna wash you off. Let me take care of everything."

He leads me into the walk-in shower. He's still fully dressed, and as soon as the water hits his clothes, it turns maroon—Deon's blood.

Knight undresses before I can freak out.

The warm water hitting my back should ease the tension that has wrapped itself around me, but it doesn't. I can still smell blood, so I know Deon is still all over me. I hysterically start pulling at my hair, trying to pull the fragments of him out of it.

"Sssh," Knight says. He grabs both of my hands and pulls me closer to him until my arms are wrapped around his waist. "I got you, Solanie."

He reaches up and pulls a bottle of shampoo down. He flips open the cap, pours some of it into his palm, and rubs his hands together. I instantly relax at the masculine smell of the shampoo because it smells just like Knight.

He runs his shampoo covered hands through my hair while never taking his eyes off mine. I wrap my arms tighter around him, never wanting to let him go. He massages my scalp and runs his fingers through my short tresses.

"I gotta rinse it out," he tells me as he reaches for the shower head attachment. I close my eyes as the warm water runs through my hair, falling onto my face. I no longer smell Deon or the scent of blood. The only thing I smell now is Knight.

He follows the shampoo with an equally masculine smelling conditioner. After rinsing it, he pours some body wash onto a sponge and runs it across my back. I wrap my arms around him even tighter, allowing him to wash every trace of Deon's death off me.

"I need you to turn around, babe," he tells me, his voice soft and gentle.

I release my grip on him, even though it's the last thing I want to do. He takes a washcloth and runs it across my face a couple of times, then down my neck. I close my eyes when he runs the body sponge across my breasts and stomach, then down my legs.

I open my eyes and stare at the water and suds flowing into the drain. Every last piece of Deon is drifting down the drain with the soap and water. I wish every memory would go down with it.

After Knight is satisfied that I'm clean, he starts washing his own body. I grab a fresh washcloth and help him, gently rubbing all over his back, making sure there are no traces of tonight still left on him.

Afterwards, he turns around and faces me. We stare at each other in silence. I wish I could read his mind. I wonder if he can read mine. He closes the distance between us in the shower and kisses me. I kiss him back with a greedy need to find some kind of relief from the pain still gripping me.

Knight grabs both sides of my face, and our kiss intensifies. He presses me up against the shower wall and lifts me up. I lock my legs around his waist. It's my turn to grasp both sides of his face. I moan into his mouth as he kisses me with fervor, reclaiming my mouth as his own.

I don't know how we got out of the shower and to the bed. But here we are, both of our bodies still wet from the shower. Knight is standing at the edge of the bed, hovering over me while taking my lips prisoner. I wrap my legs around his waist and try to pull him closer to my body.

He pulls away, and I see indecision in his eyes.

"Please," I hear myself saying. He's already washed Deon from the outside of me; now I need him to wash every trace of him from the inside of me.

"Are you sure?" Knight asks. His forehead is creased. He's not sure if he should do this. He's worried I can t handle making love right now.

"I need this, Knight. I need you to take away what he did to me."

Knight flinches.

"I need you to replace the memories of him." I cry. "Fuck every memory of him outta me."

Knight frowns before bringing his mouth to mine, infusing my lips with the taste of him. When I think I can't take it any longer, he separates our mouths. He stares into my eyes, and there goes that honesty that I've come to recognize buried deep in his eyes.

"I'm not going to fuck you tonight, Solanie." His voice is thick. "I'm going to make love to you. And when I do, I need you to know that is *exactly* what I'm doing—making love to you because I love you."

I gasp at the impact of his words. This is the first time that he's told me he loves me. I've never told him before, but I've known it since he rescued me from that burning house. Maybe I knew it even before that. For sure I know now that I'll love this man for the rest of my life.

He moves so slowly as he enters me, stopping to make sure he isn't hurting me once he sees the tears. I'm not crying because of Deon or anything he did to me. I'm crying because with every stroke Knight gives me, I can feel the power Deon had over me evaporate.

"Solanie." Knight's voice is strained. His eyes are low and locked on mine. "Please understand that what we're doing right now has nothing to do with what that motherfucka did to you. They don't correlate, baby. They're not the same thing."

I suck in air. I know Knight is trying to make sure I don't have any negative association with sex because of what Deon took from me. But there is no way I could ever confuse Knight's touch with the disgusting touch of Deon.

"Stay here with me, baby," Knight says.

I blink several times as my mind comes back to the present. Knight is trying to keep my mind from wandering to the dark things that happened to me, so I focus on his touch, his eyes, his beautiful lips. And now I have a sudden desire to kiss Knight's beautiful mouth. I need his mouth on top of mine, but I also need him to keep looking at me in the raw way that he's doing now.

"I love you," I finally tell him back.

"Give me your pain, baby."

I whimper at his words and move my hips in synchronization to the movements of his.

"You don't have to carry it anymore. It's too heavy for you. Just give it to me, baby. Let me carry it for you. Give me every broken piece of you. I'll spend the rest of my life trying to put you back together."

Knight's eyes are locked on mine as his words bare his soul. He thrusts himself inside of me, connecting our souls, removing every trace of anybody else before him. His soul pours into mine, enveloping it with all his love and a promise to protect me forever.

And I feel completely safe.

I want to stare at him all night, but the intensity of pleasure forces my eyes closed. Knight's lips kiss away every tear behind my closed lids. My legs tighten around his body. I pull him closer to me, even though there's no way we could be any closer than we are right now. Our souls intertwined. Our hearts interconnect until every broken piece of mine is put back into place.

I can feel his lips all over me. My stomach tightens with the need for a release. A guttural moan escapes my mouth, and my legs start trembling. I want this feeling to last forever, but I can tell I'm on the brink of shattering.

"That's right, baby. Let me love you." Knight's breath is warm against my neck. He kisses and sucks, and I don't even care that it'll leave a mark.

My walls clench around his length, pulsating as ripples of pleasure race dizzily all over me. My head rolls back, and my eyes follow. My mouth opens, and a long drawn-out moan rips from my chest.

The convulsion that takes over my body feels so good that it's almost painful. I suck in air, trying to fill my lungs that feel as if they've gone completely empty. I don't get the chance to catch my breath before another orgasm comes barreling out of nowhere, making me quake underneath Knight and cuss him out at the same time.

"Tell me you love me again, baby." Knight groans as his pace picks up. Egged on by my orgasms, his voice tells me he's nearing his own.

"I love you, Knight. I love you so much." I moan into his ear.

My walls clench around him, ripple against his girth, giving him permission to release himself inside of me.

"Argh," he groans. His body jerks in exhilarated spasms before he collapses on top of me.

Our breathing is heavy and in sync. He lifts up just enough to kiss me. He doesn't pull out of me, keeping us connected even though both of our bodies are spent from gratification that has exhausted us.

Skin to skin. Eye to eye. No room for anything to ever come in between us. He's mine, and I'm completely his.

KNIGHT

I catch Solanie looking over her shoulder as we pull up to my clinic. I've been doing my best to make her feel secure and safe, but this is going to be an ongoing battle. I guess I can't erase a month of torture in a week's time. But as sure as my name is Knight, I won't stop until she no longer remembers what that coward ass nigga even looked like.

"So you own this?" she asks as we get out of my truck. She's looking at my clinic as if it's something to be proud of.

"Yeah."

"You have doctors working for you and everything like that?"

"I did." I unlock the door, open it, and unarm the security system.

She frowns. "What you mean, you did?"

"I'm shutting this place down."

"Why?"

I flip on a few lights as we walk to the back toward my office. I don't know how to explain to her that I no longer want to be the man responsible for the destruction of another person. After seeing how hard Solanie fights daily to regain control of her life, there's no way I can keep ignoring the faces of people who have lost all control of their own lives.

I know I'm not the reason they're addicted to this shit. I just choose not to be the avenue through which they can easily get this shit.

"It's time for me to do something else," I finally answer her.

She's looking at me like she's all impressed, and I gluttonously feed off her admiration.

I walk behind my desk and pull out several files. I then pull the hard drive from my computer and dump it into the brown leather bag I'd brought with me.

"How long have you had this place?" Solanie wants to know.

"Too long," I answer her. And I ain't going to miss it. It's the main reason I have cops breathing down my throat, watching my every move, waiting on me to slip up. Even taking it as far as fucking with my brother to get to me. Plus, being meticulous with my every decision is exhausting. Not to mention, I've made more money here than I could ever spend in my lifetime. I'm going to do what my father wanted to do all those years ago—go completely clean.

When I look up at Solanie, all I see is the woman that's going to be my wife. I want to grow the King dynasty with her, and when she's ready, she'll have my children.

"Why you looking at me like that?" she asks when she catches me staring at her.

"Just thinking about how much I love you." It sounds funny telling a woman that I love her. I haven't ever told that to a woman other than my momma. And it ain't game when I say it to Solanie. I really mean that shit.

This is new to me, and I can tell it's all new to her too. Because she hasn't ever had a man love her the way I'm going to dedicate my life to loving her. It ain't shit I won't do for this woman, and I'm going to spend the rest of my life showing her that too.

She walks up to me, lifts her face, and smiles. "Well, I love you too, Mr. King. My Knight in shining armor."

I lean down and kiss those perfect lips. Her lipstick feels sticky and will probably leave some kind of residue on my own lips, but I don't care about any of that when I'm kissing this woman.

"Well, isn't this beautiful." Someone is clapping their hands behind us in a slow and sarcastic speed.

Solanie jumps back. Her face goes all frantic. I grab her hand to remind her that I'm here with her, and I ain't gonna let shit happen to her.

I glare at the mothafucker that's standing before us. He's dressed in a fitted suit, and he doesn't look like a fiend that's here to beg for some pills. I can tell by the smug expression on his face that he's a cop before he even pulls out that shiny ass badge.

"I'm FBI Agent Mitchell," he says. His eyes jump from me to Solanie.

Solanie is damn near trembling next to me, and I'm trying to figure out why she's so afraid.

"What the fuck do you want? I know you better have a warrant to be walking in my place of business up on me like this," I bark. I'm getting tired of these fools thinking they can stalk me, harass me, and get away with the shit. Not to mention the fact this nigga got my girl so upset.

He runs his bony ass hand over his head, his receding hairline and balding top evidence of a man that can't come to grasps with the fact that he's going bald. I look at him like he's dog shit on the bottom of my Yeezy sneakers.

"You know, my office has been building a case on you for months," he says. "We could never pin anything on you. I chalked it up as a fuckin' lost cause and just gave up on ever catching your big ass." He laughs and shakes his head. The way his facial expression changes in a split second lets me know this nigga is crazy.

Solanie squeezes my hand, and I can tell there's more to this nigga being here than him being an FBI agent after me. I move slowly, trying to assess the time it'll take me to reach the piece in the back of my waistband and unload it into his chest.

"Where's my fuckin' brother, Solanie?" he snarls.

Solanie sucks in air but doesn't say a word.

"Your brother?" I frown before realization hits me so hard, I almost double back.

"I haven't been able to reach him for days now!" Agent Mitchell's jumpy and bloodshot eyes are back on me now. "I know you killed him!"

I laugh. It's probably the wrong thing to do in the face of a crazy motherfucker like him, but I couldn't have held that laugh if I tried.

Agent Mitchell reacts to me laughing by pulling his weapon on me. His hand is unsteady though. He's jumpy and unbalanced.

He's afraid.

"You said it's Agent Mitchell, right?" I say. "And you say you've been building a case against me for months, huh? If that's the case, then I know you know exactly the kinda man I am. You gotta know your aim better be straight if you got the balls to pull a gun on me."

"Oh, the great fuckin' Knight King!" he yells. Spit is flying all out of his mouth. He's looking more like some deranged ass nutcase than an FBI agent. "Trust me, I know all about you and your fuckin' family. That's how I know my brother is already dead." His voice starts to crack.

I look at Solanie, and the fear on her face causes something inside of me to snap.

I release her hand and take it back to my football days,

charging toward Agent Mitchell headfirst. I hit him straight in his center, knocking him right off his feet. His gun goes flying in the air. I'm on top of him beating his face into the ground, ignoring the ripping of every scab on my knuckles.

I hear the moment his nose breaks against my fist. I'm not going to stop until every bone in his fucking face does the same.

"Freeze!"

I heard the order, but it takes a few seconds for my hands to stop. I look up to see that bitch that came through here about a month ago. The one who tried to entrap Kian. Another fucking FBI agent. Her gun is aimed directly at me, and her finger is on the trigger.

"Get off him!" she yells at me.

Agent Mitchell groans underneath me. I stand up and give him one last kick to the abdomen. "Pussy," I jeer at his ass.

"I said enough!"

I look at this cop broad, trying to remember her name. It's hard to think straight, knowing that this nigga is Deon's brother and he's still breathing. I would have beat him to death with my bare hands if this broad hadn't burst in here.

Why is she here anyway? Let me guess. She's a dirty cop too. I glower at her, hoping I can spot a shift in her aim, waiting for the moment to knock her ass to the ground too. I don't look over at Solanie. I don't think I can handle seeing the expression on her face right now.

"Taylor," Agent Mitchell coughs. He's holding his abdomen while trying to get to his feet. "Thank God you're here."

Yeah, that's it. Agent Taylor is her name.

"Stay down, Mitchell," she orders.

"He's The Beauty Butcher!" Solanie shouts.

Agent Taylor gives Solanie a knowing look. It's the first

time I look over at Solanie, and I'm shocked as hell to see that she's holding the pistol Agent Mitchell dropped.

"She's fuckin' crazy!" Agent Mitchell hollers in his defense.

"I know she's not lying, Mitchell," Agent Taylor says. Her gun goes from being aimed on me to him and then back again on me. "I know about your brother."

Agent Mitchell shuts his eyes like somebody just tossed something in his face. He growls and says something that sounds like nothing but gibberish.

"They killed a lot of women," Solanie says. "Both of them... He deserves to die."

"Like you killed my brother?" Agent Mitchell huffs.

"You fucking right I killed him!" Solanie admits. I wince and try to get her to look at me, but her eyes never leave Agent Mitchell. "I put four bullets in his skull. I stood there and watched his brains explode all over the room, and I loved every minute of it."

"Stay down, Mitchell," Agent Taylor roars as the nigga tries to get to his feet.

"I'd kill him a thousand times a day if I could," Solanie continues. "After everything he did to me! After everything he did to all those other women... I did the world a favor by killing his ass."

"Are you listening to her?" Agent Mitchell's eyes are on fire. "She's standing here admitting to murder! Shoot her, Taylor!"

Agent Taylor's indecision is written all over her face. Either way, we're fucked. Solanie has just confessed to an FBI agent that she murdered someone.

If we don't walk out of here in body bags, we'll be walking out of here in handcuffs.

FBI SPECIAL AGENT TAYLOR

I didn't call for backup. I didn't let anyone know where I was headed. I guess I didn't allow myself to believe what I was actually on my way to do.

I had a feeling Mitchell was going to be here. After leaving his brother's apartment, I stopped by his house and Jess told me she hadn't heard from him in hours. I knew since Knight's home is like a fortress, he wasn't going to be there. I went off a hunch that he'd be here, and I see that I arrived just in time.

If I hadn't gotten here when I did, Knight would have killed him. Not that he doesn't deserve it. I guess it just took Solanie saying it out loud for it to really hit.

I keep my gun trained on Knight. He looks like a man that's ready and willing to take a few bullets if it means he can finish Mitchell off with his bare hands.

My gun may be on Knight, but my eyes are on Mitchell. I don't recognize the man on the ground before me, and it isn't because his face is bloody and battered. He isn't the same man that I've worked alongside for four years. He isn't the man who holds the same values and honor to the badge that I do.

All this time, the city was searching for The Beauty Butcher, and one of them was working right beside me, doing everything that goes against what we stand for. I swore to protect the United States against all enemies, foreign and domestic, never once imagining the enemy would be right in my face every day for four years.

I have two choices before me now. I can arrest Mitchell and take Solanie in as well. I mean, she did just confess to first degree murder, and I swore to uphold the law. Or I could turn a blind eye...

"Taylor!" Mitchell cries out to me, like I owe him any kind of sympathy or allegiance. "Shoot her!"

I lower my weapon, and Mitchell's eyes bulge out of their sockets. The shock quickly wears off though and is replaced with a sick smile. He starts laughing, and it sounds so unnatural, so evil.

"You stupid ass bitch," he spits at me. "You've always been too stupid for your own good. I got off working next to you every day while you chased down every useless lead on The Butcher. I jacked off every night pretending I was fucking your whiney ass mouth." His voice goes high pitched as he mocks me, "Knight King this and Knight King that. We have to catch Knight King!"

I shake my head, but my confusion goes nowhere. "I don't get it. If you and your brother were the ones out here killing women, why did you keep trying to deter me from the King case? Why did you keep telling me to focus on the Butcher case?"

His laugh gets crazier. He's lying on his back, looking straight up at the ceiling. When his eyes land on me, chills run down my spine. I'm staring in the eyes of pure evil.

"Because, like I said, you've always been fuckin' stupid. You thought you were making leeway on the case, so I just let you keep thinking that. It made my dick throb knowing I was always gonna be one step ahead of your lil' dumb ass."

I close my eyes and mourn the man I thought I once knew. When I open my eyes, I give Knight a look that he quickly understands. I then turn around and leave the room like I was never there.

I get all the way to the front door before I hear two gunshots in rapid succession. I wait for guilt to hit me.

It never does.

EPILOGUE

Solanie

Nine Months Later

Cheers and applause go off all around us as Knight cuts the red ribbon in front of his new establishment: King's Alcohol and Drug Rehabilitation Center.

It's in the same building where he'd operated his pain management clinic. He never told me why he'd decided to shut it down and go in a completely different direction, but I could always see the passion in his eyes when he spoke of the plans he had for his new venture.

I look out in the crowd of smiling faces, people proud of the neighborhood's new business. None of them prouder than I am. Knight drapes his arm over my shoulder and pulls me in for a quick kiss. I'd preferred something longer and more passionate, but I understand we have an audience.

I watch him as walks into the crowd, shaking hands and hugging influential people. I notice Mariah all hugged up with Kian in the corner and smile, even though I still have reservations about them being a couple. Mariah doesn't know the things Kian is capable of, and I hope she never has to find out.

Kian catches me staring at them, and he gives me a friendly smile. We'll forever be linked together not only because we both love his brother so much, but because of the night we took a life together. I never did find out what Kian did with

Deon's body...

I never asked.

"Girl, what you over here looking all dazed out for?" Candace is by my side saying. She runs her hands through her hair and sucks her teeth. "I thought you said it was going to be a lot of single men here."

My eyes reactively go to her bare ring finger. She finally built the courage to end her engagement with James. She knew she'd never marry him and decided to stop leading him on. I heard he took it pretty hard, but according to Facebook, he's already in another relationship.

"There is," I tell her. I throw my head in the direction of the man Knight is talking to. He's an up and coming attorney trying to make his way to the DA's office.

"Ooh, he is fine," Candace says. She runs her hands over her dress as if it could even be wrinkled as tight as it is. She walks off and looks over her shoulder, winking at me.

I shake my head and decide to go inside the clinic. Ida is already inside, standing behind the receptionist desk, handing out refreshments to everybody. As soon as she sees me, her face lights up.

"Hey there, Solanie," she calls out to me

She hands me a plastic cup of punch when I walk up to her.

"I made that myself," she tells me. I sip it, and it's a delicious concoction of pineapple and coconut.

"That son of mine really did it, huh?" Ida looks around the newly remodeled waiting area. "I was against him shutting down the clinic at first. Until he told me his reasons. I couldn't argue with him after that. You know, once that man makes his mind up about something, it's a wrap." She laughs, and I laugh with her, knowing all too well how bull-headed Knight can be.

"He makes good decisions though," she adds, and something in her face tells me she's talking about me. I blush under her compliment. Knowing she approves of me means more than it should. I can't help it; I've always been intimidated by the graceful Ida King.

Our moment is interrupted by someone walking up, asking Ida all kinds of questions. I sneak off and walk down the hall. The place has been completely remodeled, and I no longer recognize the room that used to be Knight's office. The room where I'd taken another life...

I enter one of the rooms where the rehabilitation group meetings will be held. I run my hand across the rich mahogany table and envision the room one day being filled with people receiving the help that they need.

"I love what you guys have done with the place."

I turn around and see Agent Taylor standing in the doorway. She's smiling at me, so I return her warm smile.

"I never in a million years thought Knight King would open a drug rehab center," she laughs.

I don't say anything in response. I just stare at her, wishing I could read the things she isn't saying. I wonder if her decision to walk out of that room that day haunts her. If she feels responsible for her partner's death, or worse, if she feels responsible for not recognizing who he was sooner and stopping him before so many women were killed.

"Knight never ceases to amaze me," she says, fully entering the room. She walks up to me and sticks her hand out. I'm confused by the gesture, but I shake her hand anyway. "I never got to apologize," she says. "If only I'd known..."

"I've learned not to dwell on the past," I tell her. "We can never go back and change it. What we can do is concentrate on the present and the future so that we don't make the same mistakes of our past."

"Wise words," she says, and her mouth rises into a tiny smile. "Well, I better head back to the office. I just had to stop by and see the place for myself. The bureau can barely believe this place really exists."

I want to ask her if the case against Knight is still open, but something tells me it's been officially closed. Just like Kian's gun case. Just like The Beauty Butcher case. It's been months, but the media is still talking about the serial killing police captain and the sons that followed in his footsteps. The fact an FBI agent assigned to The Beauty Butchers case was actually one of the killers made for a nationwide news scandal.

His pregnant wife stayed on TV doing interviews on how she never had any idea. I used to feel bad knowing his son would grow up never knowing his father. But then I realized it's probably for the better. Nate and Deon's father passed down his sickness. It was only a matter of time before Nate passed it onto his son.

"Good luck," Agent Taylor says as she walks toward the door. "You and Knight… y'all deserve happiness."

I smile at her words as she disappears out of the room.

As soon as Agent Taylor is gone, Knight is walking into the room.

"You just missed Agent Taylor," I tell him.

He looks behind him. "I did?"

"She just wanted to see the place. She looked proud."

Knight laughs and pulls me to him. He wraps his arms around me and asks, "What about you? Are you proud of your man?"

"Very," I tell him before looking into his eyes, hoping he can see all the reasons he's made me proud, and they started long before this center was opened.

He kisses me, and heat rushes through my body. He bends

down, and I wonder if he's trying to get nasty in this conference room with all those people out there. I don't mind it one bit, but he at least needs to let me go close the door.

I give him a look, about to tell him just that, when he pulls a ring box out. He's on one knee, holding a black velvet box, and it feels like my heart is about to stop.

I gasp and cover my mouth with both of my hands.

"Solanie, I came too close to losing you. I never want to go another day without you in my life. I don't want to even imagine my life without you. I wanna wake up to you every morning and go to sleep with you every night... for the rest of my life."

I'm nodding and screaming yes before he can even ask the question.

He laughs and opens the ring box. Of course, the ring is gorgeous. He slides it onto my shaking finger, and I'm crying and blubbering like a fool.

"She said yes!" Knight calls out.

The room then quickly fills with people. Mariah and Candace are at my side in seconds.

"Girl, lemme see that ring!" Candace snatches my hand up and gawks at the size of my ring. "Now see, if James would have bought me a ring like this, I'd be married to his ass right now."

I laugh and swipe the tears from my face.

"I helped him pick it out," Mariah whispers to me.

"You did good," I tell her. I hug her and then Candace.

Ida pushes her way through everybody until she's right next to me. She hugs me and then winks at me. "Told you he makes good decisions."

Kurtis wraps her up in his burly arms and smiles at me. "Yeah, he's like his father. He knows a good woman when he sees one."

I feel like I'm about to explode on an overload of joy. I never imagined I'd be here, this happy, this fulfilled. After everything that's happened to me, I thought it'd be impossible to smile like this. To be happy like this.

Knight wraps his arm over my shoulder. I look up at him, and he leans down to kiss me. His kiss makes a promise to my heart that I know will never be broken. A love this powerful will always win. Deon may have tried to break me, but Knight put me back together.

I look at the ring on my finger through teary eyes and smile. This is really happening. I'm going to marry Knight King.

He's mine.

And I'm his.

Forever.

Made in the USA
Columbia, SC
14 October 2023

24461719R00091